COWBOY STORIES

COWBOY STORIES

Illustrated by BARRY MOSER

Introduction by PETER GLASSMAN

chronicle books · san francisco

For my good friend Jay O. Sanders —B. M.

For Jonathan, Carlie, Gabrielle, and Madeline—my favorite buckaroos! —P. G.

Book design by Barry Moser.
Cover design by Meagan Bennett.
Typesetting by Donna Linden.
Typeset in Joanna and Grit Primer.
The illustrations in this book were created with engraved blocks that were inked and printed on paper.
Manufactured in China.

Library of Congress Cataloging-in-Publication Data
Cowboy stories / illustrated by Barry Moser ; introduction by Peter Glassman.
     v. cm.
   Contents: Introduction / by Peter Glassman — From Shane / by Jack Schaefer — From Lonesome dove / by Larry McMurtry — Top hand / by Luke Short — A buffalo hunt / by Nat Love — The gift of Cochise / by Louis L'Amour — The blood bay / by Annie Proulx — Three-ten to Yuma / by Elmore Leonard — From The secret life of cowboys / by Tom Groneberg — Twelve o'clock / by Stephen Crane — From Riders of the purple sage / by Zane Grey — Shallow graves / by E. C. "Teddy Blue" Abbott — I woke up wicked / by Dorothy M. Johnson — The bandana / by J. Frank Dobie — From The Virginian / by Owen Wister — Wine on the desert / by Max Brand — From Biting the dust / by Dirk Johnson — Hewey and the wagon cook / by Elmer Kelton — From Breaking Clean / by Judy Blunt — The reformation of Calliope / by O. Henry — Long ride back / by Ed Gorman — Home on the range / by Brewster Higley.
   ISBN-13: 978-0-8118-5418-4
   ISBN-10: 0-8118-5418-3
   1. Cowboys—Juvenile fiction. 2. Children's stories, American. [1. Cowboys—Fiction.   2. Short stories.] I. Moser, Barry, ill.
   PZ5.C8385 2007
   [Fic]—dc22
   2006031568

Distributed in Canada by Raincoast Books
9050 Shaughnessy Street, Vancouver, British Columbia V6P 6E5

10 9 8 7 6 5 4 3 2 1

Chronicle Books LLC
680 Second Street, San Francisco, California 94107

www.chroniclekids.com

Contents

Introduction

BY PETER GLASSMAN

PEOPLE CITE MANY different things as being typically or uniquely American. Baseball, apple pie, and hot dogs are all considered icons of American culture. When it comes to music, jazz is widely recognized as uniquely American. Thanksgiving and the Fourth of July are viewed as classically American holidays. And when it comes to folklore, legends, and mythology, nothing is so strikingly American as the cowboy.

Anywhere in the world you go, the cowboy is seen as a symbol of America's legendary Wild West. The cowboy is remembered both as a loner—a man who lived by a strict code of honor, depended on quick wits and quicker reflexes, put his faith in his pistol and his horse, and usually let his actions speak for him—and as a member of a special fraternity whose members lived by their own rules and could not abide the restraints of domesticity or city life.

Yet, in many ways, this most American of icons has much in common with British folklore and legends. Look closely at the cowboy of the Wild West and, beneath his chaps, leather boots, and gun belt, you'll find numerous similarities between him and the Knights of the Round Table or the Merry Men of Sherwood Forest. Though no cowboy can lay claim to being the American King Arthur or Robin Hood, there are many tales about cowboys whose deeds and mannerisms link them to the men who followed these legendary leaders.

Surely, the men who rode together across the plains on cattle drives came to share a bond wrought from common purpose and shared experiences, as did the Round Table's knights and Robin Hood's men. Tales of the lone cowboy, traveling on his own and often setting what was wrong right, carry the echoes of the valiant Sir Lancelot or Sir Gawain who also ventured out on individual quests to help those in need. The gentle giant who becomes a fierce fighter in a brawl surely owes much to Little John, while the singing cowboy can be seen as the Wild West's version of Will Scarlet or Allan-a-Dale. The rascal or downright no-good cowboy who reforms himself or finds redemption certainly is following in the footsteps of Sir Kay, while wily older cowboys bring to mind the maturity and experience that Sir Pellinore and Sir Bedivere represent among King Arthur's knights. Tales of the young page who works to earn his right to be first a squire and then a knight are akin to the stories of the young lad who signs on as a cowhand, eager to prove his worth on the cattle drive and earn the respect of his fellows.

Where the knights of old had jousts and tournaments, cowboys had shootouts and pistol duels. Knights may have battled fire-breathing dragons whose mighty roars shook the earth, but cowboys faced down herds of buffalo that literally covered the prairies and whose passage just as surely set the earth to shaking. Cowboys also faced the fury of stampeding cattle—surely as dangerous a feat as facing any dragon. While a knight could be recognized by his suit of armor, so too could a cowboy be known by his hat, gun belt, chaps, and spurs. And just as the knight lived by the code of chivalry, so too did the cowboy live by a code of honor—those who violated it were disgraced in their fellows' eyes.

It would be a mistake, however, to view the tradition of the cowboy story as nothing more than older, British legends retold in a more modern, American style and setting. For the cowboy tradition is rich in its own lore. As Joseph Campbell discusses in his works on mythological traditions around the world, there are certain basic archetypes that reoccur in all mythologies and stories. The similarities between the British heroic myths and the tales of the American cowboy are due, not to imitation, but rather to both having arisen in response to similar needs.

The stories of King Arthur and his knights and Robin Hood and his Merry Men did not always enjoy the great popularity that they do today. In fact, no edition of Malory's Le Morte d'Arthur was published from 1634 until 1816, when a three-volume edition was issued. The following year, in 1817, a two-volume edition was issued by another publisher. Then, in 1819, Sir Walter Scott's

Ivanhoe was published. The appearance in that novel of Robin Hood led to a popular revival of the outlaw and his followers.

It is no coincidence that the popularity of these stories, about a king and his knights who defend the weak from the strong (who often abuse and mistreat them) and about a gang of wrongly outlawed men who rob from the rich to give to the poor, occurred on the heels of the first Industrial Revolution. Many people felt helpless against the great wealth and power of the factory owners and industrialists of this period. Tales of heroes standing up to the powerful in the name of what was right would have been a tonic to those whose way of life had been disrupted—if not shattered—by the Industrial Revolution.

It should come as no surprise, then, that as the United States experienced the pains of the second Industrial Revolution, with its stifling mills and factories and the resultant loss of individual craftsmen and artisans who could not compete with the far cheaper products from these new industrial giants, that stories of fiercely independent cowboys who roamed great tracts of open prairies, determinedly braving the challenges of both beast and nature, caught the people's imagination and grew from popular entertainment into legend and myth.

In his 22 stunning engravings, artist Barry Moser has captured the strident individualism and rugged independence that characterize the cowboys of legend and lore. How fitting that Moser's illustrations are painstakingly hand-wrought engravings—the very sort of art form that went from viable craft to lovingly preserved, but no longer economically practical, as the second Industrial Revolution brought mechanical efficiency and speed to the creation of endless lines of identical products for the marketplace, replacing handmade products in which artist and craftsman expressed their individuality.

This, then, is the reason for the enduring popularity of the cowboy story. By capturing our unquenchable need to express our individualism, our unfailing drive to test ourselves against the many challenges that nature and our fellow man throw against us, and the unending desire to see the solitary good man beat the odds against the forces of conformity and uniformity, the cowboy story touches something deep inside all of us—and always will.

From *Shane*

BY JACK SCHAEFER

WHAT PUZZLED ME MOST was something it took me nearly two weeks to appreciate. And yet it was the most striking thing of all. Shane carried no gun.

In those days guns were as familiar all through the Territory as boots and saddles. They were not used much in the valley except for occasional hunting. But they were always in evidence. Most men did not feel fully dressed without one.

We homesteaders went in mostly for rifles and shotguns when we had any shooting to do. A pistol slapping on the hip was a nuisance for a farmer. Still every man had his cartridge belt and holstered Colt to be worn when he was not working or loafing around the house. Father buckled his on whenever he rode off on any trip, even just into town, as much out of habit, I guess, as anything else.

But this Shane never carried a gun. And that was a peculiar thing because he had a gun.

I saw it once. I saw it when I was alone in the barn one day and I spotted his saddle-roll lying on his bunk. Usually he kept it carefully put away underneath. He must have forgotten it this time, for it was there in the open by the pillow. I reached to sort of feel it—and I felt the gun inside. No one was near, so I unfastened the straps and unrolled the blankets. There it was, the most beautiful-looking weapon I ever saw. Beautiful and deadly-looking.

The holster and filled cartridge belt were of the same soft black leather as the boots tucked under the bunk, tooled in the same intricate design. I knew enough to know that the gun was a single-action Colt, the same model as the Regular Army issue that was the favorite of all men in those days and that old-timers used to say was the finest pistol ever made.

This was the same model. But this was no Army gun. It was black, almost due black, with the darkness not in any enamel but in the metal itself. The grip was clear on the outer curve, shaped to the fingers on the inner curve, and two ivory plates were set into it with exquisite skill, one on each side.

The smooth invitation of it tempted your grasp. I took hold and pulled the gun out of the holster. It came so easily that I could hardly believe it was there in my hand. Heavy like Father's, it was somehow much easier to handle. You held it up to aiming level and it seemed to balance itself into your hand.

It was clean and polished and oiled. The empty cylinder, when I released the catch and flicked it, spun swiftly and noiselessly. I was surprised to see that the front sight was gone, the barrel smooth right down to the end, and that the hammer had been filed to a sharp point.

Why should a man do that to a gun? Why should a man with a gun like that refuse to wear it and show it off? And then, staring at that dark and deadly efficiency, I was again suddenly chilled, and I quickly put everything back exactly as before and hurried out into the sun.

The first chance I tried to tell Father about it. "Father," I said, all excited, "do you know what Shane has rolled up in his blankets?"

"Probably a gun."

"But—but how did you know? Have you seen it?"

"No. That's what he would have."

I was all mixed up. "Well, why doesn't he ever carry it? Do you suppose maybe it's because he doesn't know how to use it very well?"

Father chuckled like I had made a joke. "Son, I wouldn't be surprised if he could take that gun and shoot the buttons off your shirt with you awearing it and all you'd feel would be a breeze."

"Gosh agorry! Why does he keep it hidden in the barn then?"

"I don't know. Not exactly."

"Why don't you ask him?"

Father looked straight at me, very serious. "That's one question I'll never ask him. And don't you ever say anything to him about it. There are some things you don't ask a man. Not if you respect him. He's entitled to stake his

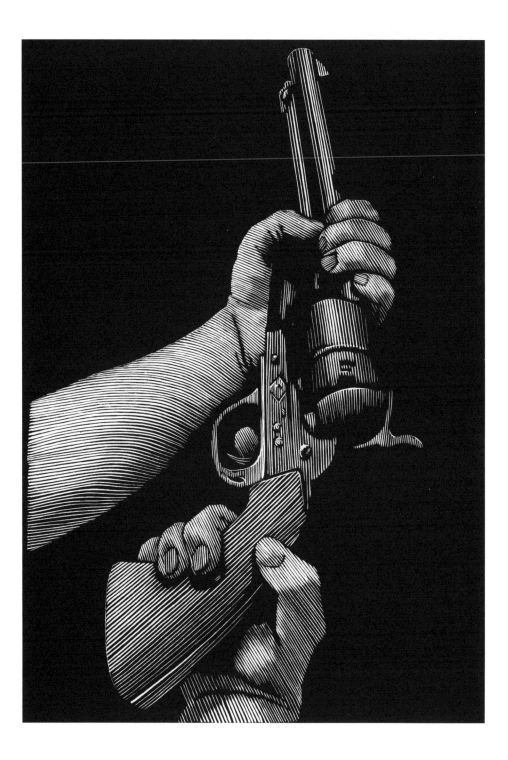

This was no Army gun.

claim to what he considers private to himself alone. But you can take my word for it, Bob, that when a man like Shane doesn't want to tote a gun, you can bet your shirt, buttons and all, he's got a mighty good reason."

———

It was plain that Shane was beginning to enjoy living with us and working the place. Little by little the tension in him was fading out. He was still alert and watchful, instinct with that unfailing awareness of everything about him. I came to realize that this was inherent in him, not learned or acquired, simply a part of his natural being. But the sharp extra edge of conscious alertness, almost of expectancy of some unknown trouble always waiting, was wearing away.

Yet why was he sometimes so strange and stricken in his own secret bitterness? Like the time I was playing with a gun Mr. Grafton gave me, an old frontier model Colt with a cracked barrel someone had turned in at the store.

I had rigged a holster out of a torn chunk of oilcloth and a belt of rope. I was stalking around near the barn, whirling every few steps to pick off a skulking Indian, when I saw Shane watching me from the barn door. I stopped short, thinking of that beautiful gun under his bunk and afraid he would make fun of me and my sorry old broken pistol. Instead he looked gravely at me.

"How many you knocked over so far, Bob?"

Could I ever repay the man? My gun was a shining new weapon, my hand steady as a rock as I drew a bead on another one.

"That makes seven."

"Indians or timber wolves?"

"Indians. Big ones."

"Better leave a few for the other scouts," he said gently. "It wouldn't do to make them jealous. And look here, Bob. You're not doing that quite right."

He sat down on an upturned crate and beckoned me over. "Your holster's too low. Don't let it drag full arm's length. Have it just below the hip, so the grip is about halfway between your wrist and elbow when the arm's hanging limp. You can take the gun then as your hand's coming up and there's still room to clear the holster without having to lift the gun too high."

"Gosh agorry! Is that the way the real gunfighters do?"

A queer light flickered in his eyes and was gone. "No. Not all of them. Most have their own tricks. One likes a shoulder holster; another packs his gun in his pants belt. Some carry two guns, but that's a show-off stunt and a waste of weight. One's enough, if you know how to use it. I've even seen a man have a tight holster with an open end and fastened on a little swivel to the belt. He didn't have to pull the gun then. Just swung up the barrel and blazed away from the hip. That's mighty fast for close work and a big target. But it's not certain past ten or fifteen paces and no good at all for putting your shot right where you want it. The way I'm telling you is as good as any and better than most. And another thing—"

He reached and took the gun. Suddenly, as for the first time, I was aware of his hands. They were broad and strong, but not heavy and fleshy like Father's. The fingers were long and square on the ends. It was funny how, touching the gun, the hands seemed to have an intelligence all their own, a sure movement that needed no guidance of thought.

His right hand closed around the grip and you knew at once it was doing what it had been created for. He hefted the old gun, letting it lie loosely in the hand. Then the fingers tightened and the thumb toyed with the hammer, testing the play of it.

While I gaped at him, he tossed it swiftly in the air and caught it in his left hand and in the instant of catching, it nestled snugly into this hand too. He tossed it again, high this time and spinning end over end, and as it came down, his right hand flicked forward and took it. The forefinger slipped through the trigger guard and the gun spun, coming up into firing position in the one unbroken motion. With him that old pistol seemed alive, not an inanimate and rusting metal object, but an extension of the man himself.

"If it's speed you're after, Bob, don't split the move into parts. Don't pull, cock, aim, and fire. Slip back the hammer as you bring the gun up and squeeze the trigger the second it's up level."

"How do you aim it, then? How do you get a sight on it?"

"No need to. Learn to hold it so the barrel's right in line with the fingers if they were out straight. You won't have to waste time bringing it high to take a sight. Just point it, low and quick and easy, like pointing a finger."

Like pointing a finger. As the words came, he was doing it. The old gun was bearing on some target over by the corral and the hammer was clicking at the empty cylinder. Then the hand around the gun whitened and the fingers slowly opened and the gun fell to the ground. The hand sank to his side, stiff and awkward. He raised his head and the mouth was a bitter gash in his face. His eyes were fastened on the mountains climbing in the distance.

"Shane! Shane! What's the matter?"

He did not hear me. He was back somewhere along the dark trail of the past.

He took a deep breath, and I could see the effort run through him as he dragged himself into the present and a realization of a boy staring at him. He beckoned to me to pick up the gun. When I did, he leaned forward and spoke earnestly.

"Listen Bob. A gun is just a tool. No better and no worse than any other tool, a shovel—or an ax or a saddle or a stove or anything. Think of it always that way. A gun is as good—and as bad—as the man who carries it. Remember that."

From *Lonesome Dove*

BY LARRY MCMURTRY

THE NEXT DAY Deets came back from his scout looking worried. "Dry as a bone, Captain," he said.

"How far did you go?"

"Twenty miles and more," Deets said.

The plain ahead was white with heat. Of course, the cattle could make twenty miles, though it would be better to wait a day and drive them at night.

"I was told if we went straight west we'd strike Salt Creek and could follow it to the Powder," Call said. "It can't be too far."

"It don't take much to be too far, in this heat," Augustus said.

"Try going due north," Call said.

Deets changed horses and left. It was well after dark when he reappeared. Call stopped the herd, and the men lounged around the wagon, playing cards. While they played, the Texas bull milled through the cows, now and then mounting one. Augustus kept one eye on his cards and one eye on the bull, keeping a loose count of his winnings and of the bull's.

"That's six he's had since we started playing," he said. "That sucker's got more stamina then me."

"More opportunity, too," Allen O'Brien observed. He had adjusted quite well to the cowboy life, but he still could not forget Ireland. When he thought of his little wife he would break into tears of homesickness, and the songs he sung to the cattle would often remind him of her.

When Deets returned it was to report that there was no water to the north. "No antelope, Captain," he said. The plains of western Nebraska had been spotted with them.

"I'll have a look in the morning," Call said. "You rest, Deets."

He found he couldn't sleep, and rose at three to saddle the Hell Bitch. Po Campo was up, stirring the coals of his cook-fire, but Call only took a cup of coffee.

"Have you been up here before?" he asked. The old cook's wanderings had been a subject of much speculation among the men. Po Campo was always letting slip tantalizing bits of information. Once, for example, he had described the great gorge of the Columbia River. Again, he had casually mentioned Jim Bridger.

"No," Po Campo said. "I don't know this country. But I'll tell you this, it is dry. Water your horse before you leave."

Call thought the old man rather patronizing—he knew enough to water a horse before setting off into a desert.

"Don't wait supper," he said.

All day he rode west, and the country around him grew more bleak. Not fit for sheep, Call thought. Not hardly fit for lizards—in fact, a small gray lizard was the only life he saw all day. That night he made a dry camp in sandy country where the dirt was light-colored, almost white. He supposed he had come some sixty miles and could not imagine that the herd would make it that far, although the Hell Bitch seemed unaffected. He slept for a few hours and went on, arriving just after sunup on the banks of Salt Creek. It was not running, but there was adequate water in scattered shallow pools. The water was not good, but it was water. The trouble was, the herd was nearly eighty miles back—a four-day drive under normal conditions; and in this case the miles were entirely waterless, which wouldn't make for normal conditions.

Call rested the mare and let her have a good roll. Then he started back and rode almost straight through, only stopping once for two hours' rest. He arrived in camp at midmorning to find most of the hands still playing cards.

When he unsaddled the mare, one of Augustus's pigs grunted at him. Both of them were lying under the wagon, sharing the shade with Lippy, who was sound asleep. The shoat was a large pig now, but travel had kept him thin. Call felt it was slightly absurd having pigs along on a cattle drive, but they had proven good foragers as well as good swimmers. They got across the rivers without any help.

Augustus was oiling his rifle. "How far did you ride that horse?" he asked.

"To the next water and back," Call said. "Did you ever see a horse like her? She ain't even tired."

"How far is it to water?" Augustus asked.

"About eighty miles," Call said. "What do you think?"

"I ain't give it no thought at all, so far," Augustus said.

"We can't just sit here," Call said.

"Oh, we could," Augustus said. "We could have stopped pretty much any-where along the way. It's only your stubbornness kept us going this long. I guess it'll be interesting to see if it can get us the next eighty miles."

Call got a plate and ate a big meal. He expected Po Campo to say something about their predicament, but the old cook merely dished out the food and said nothing. Deets was helping Pea Eye trim one of his horse's feet, a task Pea Eye had never been good at.

"Find the water, Captain?" Deets asked, smiling.

"I found it, 'bout eighty miles away," Call said.

"That's far," Pea Eye said.

They had stopped the cattle at the last stream that Deets had found, and now Call walked down it a way to think things over. He saw a gray wolf. It seemed to him to be the same wolf they had seen in Nebraska, after the picnic, but he told himself that was foolish speculation. A gray wolf wouldn't follow a cattle herd.

By midafternoon Call came back from his walk and decided they would go ahead. It was go ahead or go back, and he didn't mean to go back. It wasn't rational to think of driving cattle over eighty waterless miles, but he had learned in his years of tracking Indians that things which seemed impossible often weren't. They only became so if one thought about them too much so that fear took over. The thing to do was go. Some of the cattle might not make it, but then, he had never expected to reach Montana with every head.

He told the cowboys to push the cattle and horses onto water and hold them there.

Without saying a word, Augustus walked over, took off his clothes, and had a long bath in the little stream. The cowboys holding the herd could see him sitting in the shallow water, now and then splashing some of his long white hair.

"Sometimes I think Gus is crazy," Soupy Jones said. "Why is he sitting in the water?"

"Maybe he's fishing," Dish Boggett said facetiously. He had no opinion of Soupy Jones and saw no reason why Gus shouldn't bathe if he wanted to.

Augustus came walking back to the wagon with his hair dripping.

"It looks like sandy times ahead," he said. "Call, you got too much of the prophet in you. You're always trying to lead us into the deserts."

"Well, there's water there," Call said. "I seen it. If we can get them close enough that they can smell it, they'll go. How far do you think a cow can smell water?"

"Not no eighty miles," Augustus said.

They started the herd two hours before sundown and drove all night through the barren country. The hands had made night drives before and were glad to be traveling in the cool. Most of them expected, though, that Call would stop for breakfast, but he didn't. He rode ahead of the herd and kept on going. Some of the hands were beginning to feel empty. They kept looking hopefully for a sign that Call might slacken and let Po Campo feed them—but Call didn't slacken. They kept the cattle moving until midday, by which time some of the weaker cattle were already lagging well behind. The leaders were tired and acting fractious.

Finally Call did stop. "We'll rest a little until it starts to get cool," he said. "Then we'll drive all night again. That ought to put us close."

He wasn't sure, though. For all their effort, they had covered only some thirty-five or forty miles. It would be touch and go.

Late that afternoon, while the cowboys were lying around resting, a wind sprang up from the west. From the first, it was as hot as if it were blowing over coals. By the time Call was ready to start the herd again, the wind had risen and they faced a full-fledged sandstorm. It blew so hard that the cattle were reluctant to face it.

Newt, with the Rainey boys, was holding the drags, as usual. The wind howled across the flat plain, and the sand seemed to sing as it skimmed the ground. Newt found that looking into the wind blinded him almost instantly. He mostly ducked his head and kept his eyes shut. The horses didn't like the sand either. They began to duck and jump around, irritated at being forced into such a wind.

"This is bad luck," Augustus said to Call. He adjusted his bandana over his nose and he pulled his hat down as far as it would go.

"We can't stop here," Call said. "We ain't but halfway to water."

"Yes, and some of them will still be halfway when this blows itself out," Augustus said.

Call helped Lippy and the cook tie down everything on the wagon. Lippy, who hated wind, looked frightened; Po Campo said nothing.

"You better ride tonight," Call said to Po Campo. "If you try to walk you might get lost."

"We all might get lost tonight," Po Campo said. He took an old ax handle that he sometimes used as a cane and walked, but at least he consented to walk right with the wagon.

None of the men—no strangers to sandstorms—could remember such a sunset. The sun was like a dying coal, ringed with black long before it neared the horizon. After it set, the rim of the earth was bloodred for a few minutes, then the red was streaked with black. The afterglow was quickly snuffed out by the sand. Jasper Fant wished for the thousandth time that he had stayed in Texas. Dish Boggett was troubled by the sensation that there was a kind of river of sand flowing above his head. When he looked up in the eerie twilight, he seemed to see it, as if somehow the world had turned over and the road that ought to be beneath his feet was now over his head. If the wind stopped, he felt, the sand river would fall and bury him.

Call told them to keep as close to the cattle as possible and to keep the cattle moving. Any cattle that wandered far would probably starve to death.

Augustus thought the order foolish. "The only way to keep this herd together would be to string a rope around them—and we ain't got that much rope," he said.

Shortly after dark he was proven right. None of the animals wanted to go into the wind. It quickly became necessary for the cowboys to cover their horses' eyes with jackets or shirts; and despite the hands' precautions, little strings of cattle began to stray. Newt tried unsuccessfully to turn back two bunches, but the cattle paid him no mind, even when he bumped them with his horse. Finally he let them go, feeling guilty as he did it but not guilty enough to risk getting lost himself. He knew if he lost the herd he was probably done for; he knew it was a long way to water and he might not be able to find it, even though he was riding the good sorrel that Clara had given him.

Call felt sick with worry—the sandstorm was the worst possible luck, for it slowed down the herd and sapped the animals' strength just when they needed all they had just to reach the water. And yet there was nothing he could do about it. He tried to tie an old shirt around the Hell Bitch's eyes, but she shook him off so vigorously that he finally let it go.

At the height of the storm it seemed as if the herd might split into fragments. It was hard to see ten feet, and little bunches of cattle broke off unnoticed and slipped past the cowboys. Deets, more confident of his ability to find his way around than most, rode well west of the herd, turning back cattle whenever he found any. But it finally became pitch-dark, and even Deets could do nothing.

Augustus rode through the storm with a certain indifference, thinking of the two women he had just left. He took no interest in the straying cattle. That was Call's affair. He felt he himself deserved to be in the middle of a sandstorm on the Wyoming plain for being such a fool as to leave the women. Not a man to feel guilty, he was merely annoyed at himself for what he considered a misjudgment.

To Call's great relief, the storm blew itself out in three hours. The wind gradually died and the sand lay under their feet again instead of peppering them. The moon was soon visible, and the sky filled with bright stars. It would not be possible to judge how many cattle had strayed until the morning, but at least the main herd was still under their control.

But the storm and the long drive the day before had taken its toll in energy. By dawn, half the men were asleep in their saddles. They wanted to stop, but again Call pushed on; he knew they had lost ground and was not going to stop just because the men were sleepy. All morning he rode through the herd, encouraging the men to push the cattle. He was not sure how far they had come, but he knew they still had a full day to go. Lack of water was beginning to tell on the horses, and the weaker cattle were barely stumbling along.

Deets alone brought back most of the strayed bunches, none of which had strayed very far. The plain was so vast and flat that the cattle were visible for miles, at least to Augustus and Deets, the eyesight champions.

"There's a bunch you missed," Augustus said, pointing to the northwest. Deets looked, nodded, and rode away. Jasper Fant looked and saw nothing but heat waves and blue sky. "I guess I need spectacles," he said. "I can't see nothing but nothing."

"Weak brains breed weak eyesight," Augustus said.

"We all got weak brains or we wouldn't be here," Soupy said sourly. He had grown noticeably more discontented in recent weeks—no one knew why.

Finally at noon Call stopped. The effort to move the drags was wearing out the horses. When the cowboys got to the wagon, most of them took a cup of water and dropped sound asleep on the ground, not bothering with bedrolls or even saddle blankets. Po Campo rationed the water carefully, giving each man only three swallows. Newt felt that he could have drunk a thousand swallows. He had never tasted anything so delicious. He had never supposed plain water could be so desirable. He remembered all the times he had carelessly drunk his fill. If he ever got another chance, he meant to enjoy it more.

Call let them rest three hours and then told them to get their best mounts. Some of the cattle were so weak the cowboys had to dismount, pull their tails, and shout at them to get them up. Call knew that if they didn't make it on the next push, they would have to abandon the cattle in order to save the horses. Even after their rest, many of the cattle had their tongues hanging out. They were mulish, reluctant to move, but after much effort on the part of the exhausted men, the drive was started again.

Through the late afternoon and far into the night the cattle stumbled over the plain, the weaker cattle falling farther and farther behind. By daybreak the herd was strung out to a distance of more than five miles, most of the men plodding along as listlessly as the cattle. The day was as hot as any they remembered from south Texas—the distances that had spawned yesterday's wind refused to yield even a breeze, and it seemed to the men that the last moisture in their bodies was pouring out as sweat. They all yearned for evening and looked at the sun constantly, but the sun seemed as immobile as if suspended by a wire.

Toward midday many of the cattle began to turn back toward the water they had left two days before. Newt, struggling with a bunch, nearly got knocked off his horse by three steers that walked right into him. He noticed, to his shock, that the cattle didn't seem to see him—they were stumbling along, white-eyed. Appalled, he rode over to the Captain.

"Captain, they're going blind," he said.

The cattle had their tongues hanging out.

Call looked grim. "It ain't real blindness," he said. "They get that way when they're real thirsty. They'll try to go back to the last water."

He told the men to forget the weaker cattle and try to keep the stronger ones moving.

"We ought to make the water by night," he said.

"If we make night," Augustus said.

"We can't just stop and die," Call said.

"I don't intend to," Augustus said. "But some of the men might. That Irishman is delirious. He ain't used to such dry country."

Indeed the terrible heat had driven Allen O'Brien out of his head. Now and then he would try to sing, though his tongue was swollen and his lips cracked.

"You don't need to sing," Call said.

Allen O'Brien looked at him angrily. "I need to cry, but I've got no tears," he said. "This goddamn country has burned up my tears."

Call had been awake for over three days, and he began to feel confused himself. He knew water couldn't be much farther, but, all the same, fatigue made him doubtful. Perhaps it had been a hundred miles rather than eighty. They would never make it, if so. He tried to remember, searching his mind for details that would suggest how far the river might be, but there were precious few landmarks on the dry plain, and the harder he concentrated the more his mind seemed to slip. He was riding the Hell Bitch, but for long moments he imagined he was riding old Ben again—a mule he had relied on frequently during his campaigning on the *llano*. Ben had had an infallible sense of direction and a fine nose for water. He wasn't fast but he was sure. At the time, some men had scoffed at him for riding a mule, but Call ignored them. The stakes were life or death, and Ben was the most reliable animal he had ever seen, if far from the prettiest.

The men had had the last of Po Campo's water that morning, barely enough to wet their tongues. Po Campo doled it out with severity, careful to see that no one got more than his share. Though the old man had walked the whole distance, using his ax-handle cane, he seemed not particularly tired.

Call, though, was so tired he felt his mind slipping. Try as he might, he couldn't stay awake. Once he slept for a few steps, then jerked awake, convinced he was fighting again the battle of Fort Phantom Hill. He looked around for Indians, but saw only the thirst-blinded cattle, their long tongues hanging out, their breath rasping. His mind slipped again, and when he awoke next it was dark. The Hell Bitch was trotting. When he opened his eyes he saw the Texas bull trot past him. He reached for his reins, but they were not there. His hands were empty. Then, to his amazement, he saw that Deets had taken his reins and was leading the Hell Bitch.

No one had ever led his horse before. Call felt embarrassed. "Here, I'm awake," he said, his voice just a whisper.

Deets stopped and gave him his reins. "Didn't want you to fall and get left, Captain," he said. "The water ain't far now."

That was evident from the quickened pace of the cattle, from the way the horses began to prick their ears. Call tried to shake the sleep off, but it was as if he were stuck in it. He could see, but it took a great effort to move, and he wasn't immediately able to resume command.

Augustus loped up, seemingly fresh. "We better get everybody to the front," he said. "We'll need to try and spread them when they hit the water. Otherwise they'll all pile into the first mud-hole and tromple themselves."

Most of the cattle were too weak to run, but they broke into a trot. Call finally shook the sleep off and helped Dish and Deets and Augustus split the herd. They were only partially successful. The cattle were moving like a blind army, the scent of water in their nostrils. Fortunately they hit the river above where Call had hit it, and there was more water. The cattle spread of their own accord.

Call had not recovered from his embarrassment at having been led. Yet he knew Deets had done the right thing. He had still been dreaming of Ben and that hot day at Phantom Hill, and if he had slipped off his horse he might just have laid there and slept. But it was the first time in his life he had not been able to last through a task in command of his wits, and it bothered him.

All during the night and the next day, cattle straggled into the river, some of them cattle Call had supposed would merely become carcasses, rotting on the trail. Yet a day on the water worked wonders for them. Augustus and Dish made counts, once the stragglers stopped coming, and it appeared they had only lost six head.

The Irishman spent most of the day sitting in a puddle in Salt Creek, recovering from his delirium. He could not remember having been delirious and grew angry when the others kidded him about it. Newt, who had planned to drink all day once he got to water, soon found that he couldn't drink any more. He devoted his leisure to complicated games of mumblety-peg with the Rainey boys.

Deets went on a scout and reported that the country to the west didn't improve—grass was as scarce as water in that direction. Far to the north they could see the outlines of mountains, and there was much talk about which mountains they were.

"Why, the Rocky Mountains," Augustus said.

"Will we have to climb them?" Jasper asked. He had survived rivers and drought, but did not look forward to climbing mountains.

"No," Call said. "We'll go north, up the Powder River, right into Montana."

"How many days will it take now?" Newt asked. He had almost forgotten that Montana was a real place that they might get to someday.

"I expect three weeks or a little more and we might hit the Yellowstone," Call said.

"The Yellowstone already?" Dish Boggett said. It was the last river—or at least the last river anyone knew much about. At mention of it the whole camp fell silent, looking at the mountains.

Top Hand

By Luke Short

Gus Irby was out on the boardwalk in front of the Elite, giving his swamper hell for staving in an empty beer barrel, when the kid passed on his way to the feed stable. His horse was a good one and it was tired, Gus saw, and the kid had a little hump in his back from the cold of a mountain October morning. In spite of the ample layer of flesh that Gus wore carefully like an uncomfortable shroud, he shivered in his shirtsleeves and turned into the saloon, thinking without much interest, *Another fiddle-footed dry-country kid that's been paid off after roundup.*

Later, while he was taking out the cash for the day and opening up some fresh cigars, Gus saw the kid go into the Pride Café for breakfast, and afterward come out, toothpick in mouth, and cruise both sides of Wagon Mound's main street in aimless curiosity.

After that, Gus wasn't surprised when he looked around at the sound of the door opening, and saw the kid coming toward the bar. He was in a clean and faded shirt and looked as if he'd been cold for a good many hours. Gus said good morning and took down his best whiskey and a glass and put them in front of the kid.

"First customer in the morning gets a drink on the house," Gus announced.

"Now I know why I rode all night," the kid said, and he grinned at Gus. He was a pleasant-faced kid with pale eyes that weren't shy or sullen or bold, and maybe because of this he didn't fit readily into any of Gus's handy character pigeonholes. Gus had seen them young and fiddle-footed before, but they were the tough kids, and for a man with no truculence in him, like Gus, talking with them was like trying to pet a tiger.

Gus leaned against the back bar and watched the kid take his whiskey and wipe his mouth on his sleeve, and Gus found himself getting curious. Half a lifetime of asking skillful questions that didn't seem like questions at all prompted Gus to observe now, "If you're goin' on through you better pick up a coat. This high country's cold now."

"I figure this is far enough," the kid said.

"Oh, well, if somebody sent for you, that's different." Gus reached around lazily for a cigar.

The kid pulled out a silver dollar from his pocket and put it on the bar top, and then poured himself another whiskey, which Gus was sure he didn't want, but which courtesy dictated he should buy. "Nobody sent for me, either," the kid observed. "I ain't got any money."

Gus picked up the dollar and got change from the cash drawer and put it in front of the kid, afterward lighting his cigar. This was when the announcement came.

"I'm a top hand," the kid said quietly, looking levelly at Gus. "Who's lookin' for one?"

Gus was glad he was still lighting his cigar, else he might have smiled. If there had been a third man here, Gus would have winked at him surreptitiously; but since there wasn't, Gus kept his face expressionless, drew on his cigar a moment, and then observed gently, "You look pretty young for a top hand."

"The best cow pony I ever saw was four years old," the kid answered pointedly.

Gus smiled faintly and shook his head. "You picked a bad time. Roundup's over."

The kid nodded, drank down his second whiskey quickly, and waited for his breath to come normally. Then he said, "Much obliged. I'll see you again," and turned toward the door.

A mild cussedness stirred within Gus, and after a moment's hesitation he called out, "Wait a minute."

The kid hauled up and came back to the bar. He moved with an easy grace that suggested quickness and work-hardened muscle, and for a moment Gus,

The kid's face was young and without caution.

a careful man, was undecided. But the kid's face, so young and without caution, reassured him, and he folded his heavy arms on the bar top and pulled his nose thoughtfully. "You figure to hit all the outfits, one by one, don't you?"

The kid nodded, and Gus frowned and was silent a moment, and then he murmured, almost to himself, "I had a notion—oh, hell, I don't know."

"Go ahead," the kid said, and then his swift grin came again. "I'll try anything once."

"Look," Gus said, as if his mind were made up. "We got a newspaper here—the *Wickford County Free Press*. Comes out every Thursday, that's today." He looked soberly at the kid. "Whyn't you put a piece in there and say 'Top hand wants a job at forty dollars a month'? Tell 'em what you can do and tell 'em to come see you here if they want a hand. They'll all get it in a couple days. That way you'll save yourself a hundred miles of ridin'. Won't cost much either."

The kid thought awhile and then asked, without smiling, "Where's this newspaper at?"

Gus told him and the kid went out. Gus put the bottle away and doused the glass in water, and he was smiling slyly at his thoughts. *Wait till the boys read that in the Free Press. They were going to have some fun with that kid*, Gus reflected.

———

Johnny McSorley stepped out into the chill thin sunshine. The last silver in his pants pocket was a solid weight against his leg, and he was aware that he'd probably spend it in the next few minutes on the newspaper piece. He wondered about that, and figured shrewdly it had an off chance of working.

Four riders dismounted at a tie rail ahead and paused a moment, talking. Johnny looked them over and picked out their leader, a tall, heavy, scowling man in his middle thirties who was wearing a mackinaw unbuttoned.

Johnny stopped and said, "You know anybody lookin' for a top hand?" and grinned pleasantly at the big man.

For a second Johnny thought he was going to smile. He didn't think he'd have liked the smile, once he saw it, but the man's face settled into the scowl again. "I never saw a top hand that couldn't vote," he said.

Johnny looked at him carefully, not smiling, and said, "Look at one now, then," and went on, and by the time he'd taken two steps he thought, *Vote, huh? A man must grow pretty slow in this high country.*

He crossed the street and paused before a window marked WICKFORD COUNTY FREE PRESS, JOB PRINTING. D. MELAVEN, ED. AND PROP. He went inside, then. A girl was seated at a cluttered desk, staring at the street, tapping a pencil against her teeth. Johnny tramped over to her, noting the infernal racket made by one of two men at a small press under the lamp behind the railed-off office space.

Johnny said "Hello," and the girl turned tiredly and said, "Hello, bub." She had on a plain blue dress with a high bodice and a narrow lace collar, and she was a very pretty girl, but tired, Johnny noticed. Her long yellow hair was worn in braids that crossed almost atop her head, and she looked, Johnny thought, like a small kid who has pinned her hair up out of the way for her Saturday night bath. He thought all this and then remembered her greeting, and he reflected with rancor, *Damn, that's twice*, and he said, "I got a piece for the paper, sis."

"Don't call me sis," the girl said. "Anybody's name I don't know, I call him bub. No offense. I got that from Pa, I guess."

That's likely, Johnny thought, and he said amiably, "Any girl's name I don't know, I call her sis. I got that from ma."

The cheerful effrontery of the remark widened the girl's eyes. She held out her hand now and said with dignity, "Give it to me. I'll see it gets in next week."

"That's too late," Johnny said. "I got to get it in this week."

"Why?"

"I ain't got money enough to hang around another week."

The girl stared carefully at him. "What is it?"

"I want to put a piece in about myself. I'm a top hand, and I'm lookin' for work. The fella over there at the saloon says why don't I put a piece in the paper about wantin' work, instead of ridin' out lookin' for it."

The girl was silent a full five seconds and then said, "You don't look that simple. Gus was having fun with you."

"I figured that," Johnny agreed. "Still, it might work. If you're caught short-handed, you take anything."

The girl shook her head. "It's too late. The paper's made up." Her voice was meant to hold a note of finality, but Johnny regarded her curiously, with a maddening placidity.

"You D. Melaven?" he asked.

"No. That's Pa."

"Where's he?"

"Back there. Busy."

Johnny saw the gate in the rail that separated the office from the shop and he headed toward it. He heard the girl's chair scrape on the floor and her urgent command, "Don't go back there. It's not allowed."

Johnny looked over his shoulder and grinned and said, "I'll try anything once," and went on through the gate, hearing the girl's swift steps behind him. He halted alongside a square-built and solid man with a thatch of stiff hair more gray than black, and said, "You D. Melaven?"

"Dan Melaven, bub. What can I do for you?"

That's three times, Johnny thought, and he regarded Melaven's square face without anger. He liked the face; it was homely and stubborn and intelligent, and the eyes were both sharp and kindly. Hearing the girl stop beside him, Johnny said, "I got a piece for the paper today."

The girl put in quickly, "I told him it was too late, Pa. Now you tell him, and maybe he'll get out."

"Cassie," Melaven said in surprised protest.

"I don't care. We can't unlock the forms for every out-at-the-pants puncher that asks us. Beside, I think he's one of Alec Barr's bunch." She spoke vehemently, angrily, and Johnny listened to her with growing amazement.

"Alec who?" he asked.

"I saw you talking to him, and then you came straight over here from him," Cassie said hotly.

"I hit him for work."

"I don't believe it."

"Cassie," Melaven said grimly, "come back here a minute." He took her by the arm and led her toward the back of the shop, where they halted and engaged in a quiet, earnest conversation.

Johnny shook his head in bewilderment, and then looked around him. The biggest press, he observed, was idle. And on a stone-topped table where Melaven had been working was a metal form almost filled with lines of type and gray metal pieces of assorted sizes and shapes. Now, Johnny McSorley did not know any more than the average person about the workings of a newspaper, but his common sense told him that Cassie had lied to him when she said it was too late to accept his advertisement. Why, there was space to spare in that form for the few lines of type his message would need. Turning this over in his mind, he wondered what was behind her refusal.

Presently, the argument settled, Melaven and Cassie came back to him, and Johnny observed that Cassie, while chastened, was still mad.

"All right, what do you want printed, bub?" Melaven asked.

Johnny told him and Melaven nodded when he was finished, and said, "Pay her," and went over to the type case.

Cassie went back to the desk and Johnny followed her, and when she was seated he said, "What do I owe you?"

Cassie looked speculatively at him, her face still flushed with anger. "How much money have you got?"

"A dollar some."

"It'll be two dollars," Cassie said.

Johnny pulled out his lone silver dollar and put it on the desk. "You print it just the same; I'll be back with the rest later."

Cassie said with open malice, "You'd have it now, bub, if you hadn't been drinking before ten o'clock."

Johnny didn't do anything for a moment, and then he put both hands on the desk and leaned close to her. "How old are you?" he asked quietly.

"Seventeen."

"I'm older'n you," Johnny murmured. "So the next time you call me 'bub,' I'm goin' to take down your pigtails and pull 'em. I'll try anything once."

Once he was in the sunlight, crossing toward the Elite, he felt better. He smiled—partly at himself but mostly at Cassie. She was a real spitfire, kind of pretty and kind of nice, and he wished he knew what her father said to her that made her so mad, and why she'd been mad in the first place.

Gus was breaking out a new case of whiskey and stacking bottles against the back mirror as Johnny came in and went up to the bar. Neither of them spoke while Gus finished, and Johnny gazed absently at the poker game at one of the tables and now yawned sleepily.

Gus said finally, "You get it in all right?"

Johnny nodded thoughtfully and said, "She mad like that at everybody?"

"Who? Cassie?"

"First she didn't want to take the piece, but her old man made her. Then she charges me more for it than I got in my pocket. Then she combs me over like I got my head stuck in the cookie crock for drinkin' in the morning. She calls me bub, to boot."

"She calls everybody bub."

"Not me no more," Johnny said firmly, and yawned again.

Gus grinned and sauntered over to the cash box. When he came back he put ten silver dollars on the bar top and said, "Pay me back when you get your job. And I got rooms upstairs if you want to sleep."

Johnny grinned. "Sleep, Hunh? I'll try anything once." He took the money, said "Much obliged," and started away from the bar and then paused. "Say, who's this Alec Barr?"

Johnny saw Gus's eyes shift swiftly to the poker game and then shuttle back to him. Gus didn't say anything.

"See you later," Johnny said.

He climbed the stairs whose entrance was at the end of the bar, wondering why Gus was so careful about Alec Barr.

A gunshot somewhere out in the street woke him. The sun was gone from the room. *So it must be afternoon,* he thought. He pulled on his boots, slopped some water into the washbowl and washed up, pulled hand across his cheek and decided he should shave, and went downstairs. There wasn't anybody in the saloon, not even behind the bar. On the tables and on the bar top, however, were several newspapers, all fresh. He was reminded at once that he was in debt to the *Wickford County Free Press* for the sum of one dollar. He pulled one of the newspapers toward him and turned to the page where all the advertisements were.

When, after some minutes, he finished, he saw that his advertisement was not there. A slow wrath grew in him as he thought of the girl and her father taking his money, and when it had come to full flower, he went out of the Elite and cut across toward the newspaper office. He saw, without really noticing it, the group of men clustered in front of the store across from the newspaper office. He swung under the tie rail and reached the opposite boardwalk just this side of the newspaper office and a man who was lounging against the building. He was a puncher and when he saw Johnny heading up the walk he said, "Don't go across there."

Johnny said grimly, "You stop me," and went on, and he heard the puncher say, "All right, getcher head blown off."

His boots crunched broken glass in front of the office and he came to a gingerly halt, looking down at his feet. His glance raised to the window, and he saw where there was a big jag of glass out of the window, neatly wiping out the WICKFORD except for the "W" on the sign and ribboning cracks to all four corners of the frame. His surprise held him motionless for a moment, and then he heard a voice calling from across the street, "Clear out of there, son."

That makes four times, Johnny thought resignedly, and he glanced across the street and saw Alec Barr, several men clotted around him, looking his way.

Johnny went on and turned into the newspaper office and it was like walking into a dark cave. The lamp was extinguished.

And then he saw the dim forms of Cassie Melaven and her father back of the railing beside the job press, and the reason for his errand came back to him with a rush. Walking through the gate, he began firmly, "I got a dollar owed—" and ceased talking and halted abruptly. There was a six-shooter in Dan Melaven's hand hanging at his side. Johnny looked at it, and then raised his glance to Melaven's face and found the man watching him with a bitter amusement in his eyes. His glance shuttled to Cassie, and she was looking at him as if she didn't see him, and her face seemed very pale in that gloom. He half gestured toward the gun and said, "What's that for?"

"A little trouble, bub," Melaven said mildly. "Come back for your money?"

"Yeah," Johnny said slowly.

Suddenly it came to him, and he wheeled and looked out through the broken window and saw Alec Barr across the street in conversation with two men, his own hands, Johnny supposed. That explained the shot that wakened him. A little trouble.

He looked back at Melaven now in time to hear him saying to Cassie, "Give him his money."

Cassie came past him to the desk and pulled open a drawer and opened the cash box. While she was doing, it, Johnny strolled soberly over to the desk. She gave him the dollar and he took it, and their glances met. *She's been crying,* he thought, with a strange distress.

"That's what I tried to tell you," Cassie said. "We didn't want to take your money, but you wouldn't have it. That's why I was so mean."

"What's it all about?" Johnny asked soberly.

"Didn't you read the paper?"

Johnny shook his head in negation, and Cassie said dully, "It's right there on page one. There's a big chunk of government land out on Artillery Creek coming up for sale. Alec Barr wanted it, but he didn't want anybody bidding against him. He knew Pa would have to publish a notice of sale. He tried to get Pa to hold off publication of the date of sale until it would be too late for other bidders to make it. Pa was to get a piece of the land in return for the favor, or money. I guess we needed it all right, but Pa told him no."

Johnny looked over at Melaven, who had come up to the rail now and was listening. Melaven said, "I knew Barr'd be in today with his bunch, and they'd want a look at a pull sheet before the press got busy, just to make sure the notice wasn't there. Well, Cassie and Dad Hopper worked with me all last night to turn out the real paper, with the notice of sale and a front-page editorial about Barr's proposition to me, to boot."

"We got it printed and hid it out in the shed early this morning," Cassie explained.

Melaven grinned faintly at Cassie, and there was a kind of open admiration for the job in the way he smiled. He said to Johnny now, "So what you saw in the forms this mornin' was a fake, bub. That's why Cassie didn't want your money. The paper was already printed." He smiled again, that rather proud smile. "After you'd gone, Barr came in. He wanted a pull sheet and we gave it to him, and he had a man out front watching us most of the morning. But he pulled him off later. We got the real paper out of the shed on to the Willow Valley stage, and we got it delivered all over town before Barr saw it."

Johnny was silent a moment, thinking this over. Then he nodded toward the window. "Barr do that?"

"I did," Melaven said quietly. "I reckon I can keep him out until someone in this town gets the guts to run him off."

Johnny looked down at the dollar in his hand and stared at it a moment and put it in his pocket. When he looked up at Cassie, he surprised her watching him, and she smiled a little, as if to ask forgiveness.

Johnny said, "Want any help?" to Melaven, and the man looked at him thoughtfully and then nodded. "Yes. You can take Cassie home."

"Oh, no," Cassie said. She backed away from the desk and put her back against the wall, looking from one to the other. "I don't go. As long as I'm here, he'll stay there."

"Sooner or later, he'll come in," Melaven said grimly. "I don't want you hurt."

"Let him come," Cassie said stubbornly. "I can swing a wrench better than some of his crew can shoot."

"Please go with him."

Cassie shook her head. "No, Pa. There's some men left in this town. They'll turn up."

Melaven said "Hell," quietly, angrily, and went back into the shop. Johnny and the girl looked at each other for a long moment, and Johnny saw the fear in her eyes. She was fighting it, but she didn't have it licked, and he couldn't blame her. He said, "If I'd had a gun on me, I don't reckon they'd of let me in here, would they?"

"Don't try it again," Cassie said. "Don't try the back either. They're out there."

Johnny said, "Sure you won't come with me?"

"I'm sure."

"Good," Johnny said quietly. He stepped outside and turned up-street, glancing over at Barr and the three men with him who were watching him wordlessly. The man leaning against the building straightened up and asked, "She comin' out?"

"She's thinkin' it over," Johnny said.

The man called across the street to Barr, "She's thinkin' it over," and Johnny headed obliquely across the wide street toward the Elite. *What kind of a town is this, where they'd let this happen?* he thought angrily, and then he caught sight of Gus Irby standing under the wooden awning in front of the Elite, watching the show. Everybody else was doing the same thing. A man behind Johnny yelled, "Send her out, Melaven," and Johnny vaulted up onto the boardwalk and halted in front of Gus.

"What do you aim to do?" he asked Gus.

"Mind my own business, same as you," Gus growled, but he couldn't hold Johnny's gaze.

There was shame in his face, and when Johnny saw it his mind was made up. He shouldered past him and went into the Elite and saw it was empty. He stepped behind the bar now and, bent over so he could look under it, slowly traveled down it. Right beside the beer taps he found what he was looking for. It was a sawed-off shotgun and he lifted it up, broke it, and saw that both barrels were loaded. Standing motionless, he thought about this now, and presently he moved on toward the back and went out the rear door. It opened onto an alley, and he turned left and went up it, thinking, *It was brick, and the one next to it was painted brown, at least in front.* And then he saw it up ahead, a low brick store with a big loading platform running across its rear.

He went up to it and looked down the narrow passageway he'd remembered was between this building and the brown one beside it. There was a small areaway here, this end cluttered with weeds and bottles and tin cans. Looking through it he could see a man's elbow and segment of leg at the boardwalk, and he stepped as noiselessly as he could over the trash and worked forward to the boardwalk.

At the end of the areaway, he hauled up and looked out and saw Alec Barr some ten feet to his right and teetering on the edge of the high boardwalk, gun in hand. He was engaged in low conversation with three other men on either side of him. There was a supreme insolence in the way he exposed himself, as if he knew Melaven would not shoot at him and could not hit him if he did.

Johnny raised the shotgun hip high and stepped out and said quietly, "Barr, you goin' to throw away that gun and get on your horse or am I goin' to burn you down?"

The four men turned slowly, not moving anything except their heads. It was Barr whom Johnny watched, and he saw the man's bold baleful eyes gauge his chances and decline the risk, and Johnny smiled. The three other men were watching Barr for a clue to their moves.

Johnny said "Now," and on the heel of it he heard the faint clatter of a kicked tin can in the areaway behind him. He lunged out of the areaway just as a pistol shot erupted with a savage roar between the two buildings.

Barr half turned now with the swiftness with which he lifted his gun across his front, and Johnny, watching him, didn't even raise the shotgun in his haste; he let go from the hip. He saw Barr rammed off the high boardwalk into the tie rail, and heard it crack and splinter and break with the big man's weight, and then Barr fell in the street out of sight.

The three other men scattered into the street, running blindly for the opposite sidewalk. And at the same time, the men who had been standing in front of the buildings watching this now ran toward Barr, and Gus Irby was in the van. Johnny poked the shotgun into the areaway and without even taking sight he pulled the trigger and listened to the bellow of the explosion and the rattling raking of the buckshot as it caromed between the two buildings. Afterward, he turned down the street and let Gus and the others run past him, and he went into the Elite.

It was empty, and he put the shotgun on the bar and got himself a glass of water and stood there drinking it, thinking, *I feel some different, but not much.*

He was still drinking water when Gus came in later. Gus looked at him long and hard, as he poured himself a stout glass of whiskey and downed it. Finally, Gus said, "There ain't a right thing about it, but they won't pay you a bounty for him. They should."

Johnny didn't say anything, only rinsed out his glass.

"Melaven wants to see you," Gus said then.

"All right." Johnny walked past him and Gus let him get past him ten feet, and then said, "Kid, look."

Johnny halted and turned around and Gus, looking sheepish, said, "About that there newspaper piece. That was meant to be a rawhide, but damned if it didn't backfire on me."

Johnny just waited, and Gus went on. "You remember the man that was standing this side of Barr? He works for me, runs some cows for me. Did, I mean, because he stood there all afternoon sickin' Barr on Melaven. You want his job? Forty a month, top hand."

"Sure," Johnny said promptly.

Gus smiled expansively and said, "Let's have a drink on it."

"Tomorrow," Johnny said. "I don't aim to get a reputation for drinkin' all day long."

Gus looked puzzled and then laughed. "Reputation? Who with? Who knows—" His talk faded off, and then he said quietly, "Oh."

Johnny waited long enough to see if Gus would smile, and when Gus didn't, he went out. Gus didn't smile after he'd gone either.

A Buffalo Hunt

By Nat Love

When there was not much doing around the ranch, we boys would get up a buffalo hunt. Buffalo were plentiful in those days and one did not have to ride far before striking a herd. Going out on the open plain, we were not long in sighting a herd, peacefully grazing on the luxuriant grass, and it would have been an easy task to shoot them but that was not our idea of sport. In the first place it was too easy. Then to shoot them would rob the hunt of all elements of danger and excitement, for that reason we prepared to rope them and then dispatch them with the knife or revolver. As soon as the herd caught sight of us they promptly proceeded to stampede and were off like the wind. We all had pretty good mounts and we started in pursuit. It is a grand sight to see a large herd of several thousand buffalo on a stampede, all running with their heads down and their tongues hanging out like a yard of red flannel, snorting and bellowing they crowd along, shaking the ground for yards around. We soon reached the rear of the herd and began operations. I had roped and dispatched several, when my attention was attracted by a magnificent bull buffalo, which I made up my mind to get, running free behind the herd. My buffalo soon came within range and my rope settled squarely over his horns and my horse braced himself for the strain, but the bull proved too much for us. My horse was knocked down, the saddle snatched from under me and off my horse's back, and my neck nearly broken as I struck the hardest spot in that part of Texas. After I got through counting the stars, not to mention the moons, that I could

The bull proved too much for us.

see quite plainly, I jumped to my feet and, after assuring myself that I was all there, I looked for my horse: he was close by just getting up while, in the distance and fast growing more distant each moment, was my favorite saddle flying in the breeze, hanging to the head of the infuriated buffalo.

Now I did not think I could very well lose that saddle, so I sprang on my horse's bare back and started in pursuit. My horse could run like a deer and his hard fall did not seem to affect him much, so it did not take us long to overtake the plunging herd. Running my horse close up by the side of the thief who stole my saddle, I placed the muzzle of my forty-five close against his side and right there I took charge of Mr. Buffalo and my outfit.

It was no trouble to get all the buffalo meat we wanted in those days, all that was necessary was to ride out on the prairie and knock them over with a bullet, a feat that any cowboy can accomplish without useless waste of ammunition, and a running buffalo furnishes perhaps the best kind of a moving target for practice shooting. And the man that can drop his buffalo at two hundred yards the first shot can hit pretty much anything he shoots at.

I never missed anything I shot at within this distance and many a time when I thought the distance of an object was too great, the boys have encouraged me by saying, shoot, you never miss, and as much to my surprise as theirs, my old standby placed the bullet where I aimed.

I early in my career recognized the fact that a cowboy must know how to use his guns, and therefore I never lost an opportunity to improve my shooting abilities, until I was able to hit anything within range of my forty-five or my Winchester. This ability has times without number proved of incalculable value to me when in tight places. It has often saved the life of myself and companions, and so by constant practice I soon became known as the best shot in the Arizona and panhandle country.

The Gift of Cochise

By Louis L'Amour

Tense, and white to the lips, Angie Lowe stood in the door of her cabin with a double-barreled shotgun in her hands. Beside the door was a Winchester '73, and on the table inside the house were two Walker Colts.

Facing the cabin were twelve Apaches on ragged calico ponies, and one of the Indians had lifted his hand palm outward. The Apache sitting the white-splashed bay pony was Cochise.

Beside Angie were her seven-year-old son, Jimmy, and her five-year-old daughter, Jane.

Cochise sat his pony in silence, his black, unreadable eyes studied the woman, the children, the cabin, and the small garden. He looked at the two ponies in the corral and the three cows. His eyes strayed to the small stack of hay cut from the meadow, and to the few steers farther up the canyon.

Three times the warriors of Cochise had attacked this solitary cabin and three times they had been turned back. In all, they had lost seven men, and three had been wounded. Four ponies had been killed. His braves reported that there was no man in the house, only a woman and two children, so Cochise had come to see for himself this woman who was so certain a shot with a rifle and who killed his fighting men.

These were some of the same fighting men who had outfought, out-guessed, and outrun the finest American army on record, an army outnumbering the Apaches by a hundred to one. Yet a lone woman with two small children had fought them off, and the woman was scarcely more than a girl. And she was prepared to fight now. There was a glint of admiration in the old eyes that appraised her. The Apache was a fighting man, and he respected fighting blood.

"Where is your man?"

"He has gone to El Paso." Angie's voice was steady, but she was frightened as she had never been before. She recognized Cochise from descriptions, and she knew that if he decided to kill or capture her it would be done. Until now, the sporadic attacks she had fought off had been those of casual bands of warriors who raided her in passing.

"He has been gone a long time. How long?"

Angie hesitated, but it was not in her to lie. "He has been gone four months."

Cochise considered that. No one but a fool would leave such a woman, or such fine children. Only one thing could have prevented his return. "Your man is dead," he said.

Angie waited, her heart pounding with heavy, measured beats. She had guessed long ago that Ed had been killed, but the way Cochise spoke did not imply that Apaches had killed him, only that he must be dead or he would have returned.

"You fight well," Cochise said. "You have killed my young men."

"Your young men attacked me." She hesitated then added, "They stole my horses."

"Your man is gone. Why do you not leave?"

Angie looked at him with surprise. "Leave? Why, this is my home. This land is mine. This spring is mine. I shall not leave."

"This was an Apache spring," Cochise reminded her reasonably.

"The Apache lives in the mountains," Angie replied. "He does not need this spring. I have two children, and I do need it."

"But when the Apache comes this way, where shall he drink? His throat is dry and you keep him from water."

The very fact that Cochise was willing to talk raised her hopes. There had been a time when the Apache made no war on the white man. "Cochise speaks with a forked tongue," she said. "There is water yonder." She gestured toward the hills, where Ed had told her there were springs. "But if the people of Cochise come in peace, they may drink at this spring."

The Apache leader smiled faintly. Such a woman would rear a nation of warriors. He nodded at Jimmy. "The small one—does he also shoot?"

"He does," Angie said proudly, "and well, too!" She pointed at an upthrust leaf of prickly pear. "Show them, Jimmy."

The prickly pear was an easy two hundred yards away, and the Winchester was long and heavy, but he lifted it eagerly and steadied it against the doorjamb as his father had taught him, held his sight an instant, then fired. The bud on top of the prickly pear disintegrated.

There were grunts of appreciation from the dark-faced warriors. Cochise chuckled.

"The little warrior shoots well. It is well you have no man. You might raise an army of little warriors to fight my people."

"I have no wish to fight your people," Angie said quietly. "Your people have your ways, and I have mine. I live in peace when I am left in peace. I did not think," she added with dignity, "that the great Cochise made war on women!"

The Apache looked at her, then turned his pony away. "My people will trouble you no longer," he said. "You are the mother of a strong son."

"What about my two ponies?" she called after him. "Your young men took them from me."

Cochise did not turn or look back, and the little cavalcade of riders followed him away. Angie stepped back into the cabin and closed the door. Then she sat down abruptly, her face white, the muscles in her legs trembling.

When morning came, she went cautiously to the spring for water. Her ponies were back in the corral. They had been returned during the night.

Slowly, the days drew on. Angie broke a small piece of the meadow and planted it. Alone, she cut hay in the meadow and built another stack. She saw Indians several times, but they did not bother her. One morning, when she opened her door, a quarter of antelope lay on the step, but no Indian was in sight. Several times, during the weeks that followed, she saw moccasin tracks near the spring.

Once, going out at daybreak, she saw an Indian girl dipping water from the spring. Angie called to her, and the girl turned quickly, facing her. Angie walked toward her, offering a bright red silk ribbon. Pleased at the gift, the Apache girl left.

And the following morning there was another quarter of antelope on her step—but she saw no Indian.

Ed Lowe had built the cabin in West Dog Canyon in the spring of 1871, but it was Angie who chose the spot, not Ed. In Santa Fe they would have told you that Ed Lowe was good-looking, shiftless, and agreeable. He was, also, unfortunately handy with a pistol.

Angie's father had come from County Mayo to New York and from New York to the Mississippi, where he became a tough, brawling, river boatman. In New Orleans, he met a beautiful Cajun girl and married her. Together, they started west for Santa Fe, and Angie was born en route. Both parents died of cholera when Angie was fourteen. She lived with an Irish family for the following three years, then married Ed Lowe when she was seventeen.

Santa Fe was not good for Ed, and Angie kept after him until they started south. It was Apache country, but they kept on until they reached the old Spanish ruin in West Dog. Here there were grass, water, and shelter from the wind.

There was fuel, and there were piñons and game. And Angie, with an Irish eye for the land, saw that it would grow crops.

The house itself was built on the ruins of the old Spanish building, using the thick walls and the floor. The location had been admirably chosen for defense. The house was built in a corner of the cliff, under the sheltering overhang, so that approach was possible from only two directions, both covered by an easy field of fire from the door and windows.

For seven months, Ed worked hard and steadily. He put in the first crop, he built the house, and proved himself a handy man with tools. He repaired the old plow they had bought, cleaned out the spring, and paved and walled it with slabs of stone. If he was lonely for the carefree companions of Santa Fe, he gave no indication of it. Provisions were low, and when he finally started off to the south, Angie watched him go with an ache in her heart.

She did not know whether she loved Ed. The first flush of enthusiasm had passed, and Ed Lowe had proved something less than she had believed. But he had tried, she admitted. And it had not been easy for him. He was an amiable soul, given to whittling and idle talk, all of which he missed in the loneliness of the Apache country. And when he rode away, she had no idea whether she would ever see him again. She never did.

Santa Fe was far and away to the north, but the growing village of El Paso was less than a hundred miles to the west, and it was there Ed Lowe rode for supplies and seed.

He had several drinks—his first in months—in one of the saloons. As the liquor warmed his stomach, Ed Lowe looked around agreeably. For a moment, his eyes clouded with worry as he thought of his wife and children back in Apache country, but it was not in Ed Lowe to worry for long. He had another drink and leaned on the bar, talking to the bartender. All Ed had ever asked of life was enough to eat, a horse to ride, an occasional drink, and companions to talk with. Not that he had anything important to say. He just liked to talk.

Suddenly a chair grated on the floor, and Ed turned. A lean, powerful man with a shock of uncut black hair and a torn, weather-faded shirt stood at bay. Facing him across the table were three hard-faced young men, obviously brothers.

Ches Lane did not notice Ed Lowe watching from the bar. He had eyes only for the men facing him. "You done that deliberate!" The statement was a challenge.

The broad-chested man on the left grinned through broken teeth. "That's right, Ches, I done it deliberate. You killed Dan Tolliver on the Brazos."

"He made the quarrel." Comprehension came to Ches. He was boxed, and by three of the fighting, blood-hungry Tollivers.

"Don't make no difference," the broad-chested Tolliver said. "'Who sheds a Tolliver's blood, by a Tolliver's hand must die!'"

Ed Lowe moved suddenly from the bar. "Three to one is long odds," he said, his voice low and friendly. "If the gent in the corner is willin', I'll side him."

Two Tollivers turned toward him. Ed Lowe was smiling easily, his hand hovering near his gun. "You stay out of this!" one of the brothers said harshly.

"I'm in," Ed replied. "Why don't you boys light a shuck?"

"No, by—!" The man's hand dropped for his gun, and the room thundered with sound.

Ed was smiling easily, unworried as always. His gun flashed up. He felt it leap into his hand, saw the nearest Tolliver smashed back, and he shot him again as he dropped. He had only time to see Ches Lane with two guns out and another Tolliver down when something struck him through the stomach and he stepped back against the bar, suddenly sick.

The sound stopped, and the room was quiet, and there was the acrid smell of powder smoke. Three Tollivers were down and dead, and Ed Lowe was dying. Ches Lane crossed to him.

"We got 'em," Ed said, "we sure did. But they got me."

Suddenly his face changed. "Oh Lord in heaven, what'll Angie do?" And then he crumpled over on the floor and lay still, the blood staining his shirt and mingling with the sawdust.

Stiff-faced, Ches looked up. "Who was Angie?" he asked.

"His wife," the bartender told him. "She's up northeast somewhere, in Apache country. He was tellin' me about her. Two kids, too."

Ches Lane stared down at the crumpled, used-up body of Ed Lowe. The man had saved his life.

One he could have beaten, two he might have beaten; three would have killed him. Ed Lowe, stepping in when he did, had saved the life of Ches Lane.

"He didn't say where?"

"No."

Ches Lane shoved his hat back on his head. "What's northeast of here?"

The bartender rested his hands on the bar. "Cochise," he said. . . .

For more than three months, whenever he could rustle the grub, Ches Lane quartered the country over and back. The trouble was, he had no lead to the location of Ed Lowe's homestead. An examination of Ed's horse revealed nothing. Lowe had bought seed and ammunition, and the seed indicated a good water supply, and the ammunition implied trouble. But in the country there was always trouble.

A man had died to save his life, and Ches Lane had a deep sense of obligation. Somewhere that wife waited, if she was still alive, and it was up to him to find her and look out for her. He rode northeast, cutting for sign, but found none. Sandstorms had wiped out any hope of back-trailing Lowe. Actually, West Dog Canyon was more east than north, but this he had no way of knowing.

North he went, skirting the rugged San Andreas Mountains. Heat baked him hot, dry winds parched his skin. His hair grew dry and stiff and alkali-whitened. He rode north, and soon the Apaches knew of him. He fought them at a lonely water hole, and he fought them on the run. They killed his horse, and he switched his saddle to the spare and rode on. They cornered him in the rocks, and he killed two of them and escaped by night.

They trailed him through the White Sands, and he left two more for dead. He fought fiercely and bitterly and would not be turned from his quest. He turned east through the lava beds and still more east to the Pecos. He saw only two white men, and neither knew of a white woman.

The bearded man laughed harshly. "A woman alone? She wouldn't last a month! By now the Apaches got her, or she's dead. Don't be a fool! Leave this country before you die here."

Lean, wind-whipped, and savage, Ches Lane pushed on. The Mescaleros concerned him in Rawhide Draw and he fought them to a standstill. Grimly, the Apaches clung to his trail.

The sheer determination of the man fascinated them. Bred and born in a rugged and lonely land, the Apaches knew the difficulties of survival; they knew how a man could live, how he must live. Even as they tried to kill this man, they loved him, for he was one of their own.

Lane's jeans grew ragged. Two bullet holes were added to the old black hat. The slicker was torn; the saddle, so carefully kept until now, was scratched by gravel and brush. At night he cleaned his guns and by day he scouted the trails. Three times he found lonely ranch houses burned to the ground, the buzzard- and coyote-stripped bones of their owners lying nearby.

Once he found a covered wagon, its canvas flopping in the wind, a man lying sprawled on the seat with a pistol near his hand. He was dead and his wife was dead, and their canteens rattled like empty skulls.

Leaner every day, Ches Lane pushed on. He camped one night in a canyon near some white oaks. He heard a hoof click on stone and he backed away from his tiny fire, gun in hand.

The riders were white men, and there were two of them. Joe Tompkins and Wiley Lynn were headed west, and Ches Lane could have guessed why. They were men he had known before, and he told them what he was doing.

Lynn chuckled. He was a thin-faced man with lank yellow hair and dirty fingers. "Seems a mighty strange way to get a woman. There's some as comes easier."

"This ain't for fun," Ches replied shortly. "I got to find her."

Tompkins stared at him. "Ches, you're crazy! That gent declared himself in of his own wish and desire. Far's that goes, the gal's dead. No woman could last this long in Apache country."

At daylight, the two men headed west, and Ches Lane turned south.

Antelope and deer are curious creatures, often led to their death by curiosity. The longhorn, soon going wild on the plains, acquires the same characteristic. He is essentially curious. Any new thing or strange action will bring his head up and his ears alert. Often a longhorn, like a deer, can be lured within a stone's throw by some queer antic, by a handkerchief waving, by a man under a hide, by a man on foot.

This character of the wild things holds true of the Indian. The lonely rider who fought so desperately and knew the desert so well soon became a subject of gossip among the Apaches. Over the fires of many a *rancheria*, they discussed this strange rider who seemed to be going nowhere, but always riding, like a lean wolf dog on a trail. He rode across the *mesas* and down the canyons; he studied sign at every water hole; he looked long from every ridge. It was obvious to the Indians that he searched for something—but what?

Cochise had come again to the cabin in West Dog Canyon. "Little warrior too small," he said, "too small for hunt. You join my people. Take Apache for man."

"No." Angie shook her head. "Apache ways are good for the Apache, and the white man's ways are good for white men—and women."

They rode away and said no more, but that night, as she had on many other nights after the children were asleep, Angie cried. She wept silently, her head pillowed on her arms. She was as pretty as ever, but her face was thin, showing the worry and struggle of the months gone by, the weeks and months without hope.

The crops were small but good. Little Jimmy worked beside her. At night, Angie sat alone on the steps and watched the shadows gather down the long canyon, listening to the coyotes yapping from the rim of the Guadalupes, hearing the horses blowing in the corral. She watched, still hopeful, but now she knew that Cochise was right: Ed would not return.

But even if she had been ready to give up this, the first home she had known, there could be no escape. Here she was protected by Cochise. Other Apaches from other tribes would not so willingly grant her peace.

At daylight she was up. The morning air was bright and balmy, but soon it would be hot again. Jimmy went to the spring for water, and when breakfast was over, the children played while Angie sat in the shade of a huge old cottonwood and sewed. It was a Sunday, warm and lovely. From time to time, she lifted her eyes to look down the canyon, half smiling at her own foolishness.

The hard-packed earth of the yard was swept clean of dust; the pans hanging on the kitchen wall were neat and shining. The children's hair had been clipped, and there was a small bouquet on the kitchen table.

After a while, Angie put aside her sewing and changed her dress. She did her hair carefully, and then, looking in her mirror, she reflected with sudden pain that she was pretty, and that she was only a girl.

Resolutely, she turned from the mirror and, taking up her Bible, went back to the seat under the cottonwood. The children left their playing and came to her, for this was a Sunday ritual, their only one. Opening the Bible, she read slowly,

". . . though I walk through the valley of the shadow of death, I will fear no evil; for thou art with me; thy rod and thy staff, they comfort me. Thou preparest a table before me in the presence of mine enemies: thou . . ."

"Mommy." Jimmy tugged at her sleeve. "Look!"

———

Ches Lane had reached a narrow canyon by midafternoon and decided to make camp. There was small possibility he would find another such spot, and he was dead tired, his muscles sodden with fatigue. The canyon was one of those unexpected gashes in the cap rock that gave no indication of its presence until you came right on it. After some searching, Ches found a route to the bottom and made camp under a wind-hollowed overhang. There was water, and there was a small patch of grass.

After his horse had a drink and a roll on the ground, it began cropping eagerly at the rich, green grass, and Ches built a smokeless fire of some ancient driftwood in the canyon bottom. It was his first hot meal in days, and when he had finished he put out his fire, rolled a smoke, and leaned back contentedly.

Before darkness settled, he climbed to the rim and looked over the country. The sun had gone down, and the shadows were growing long. After a half hour of study, he decided there was no living thing within miles, except for the usual desert life. Returning to the bottom, he moved his horse to fresh grass, then rolled in his blanket. For the first time in a month, he slept without fear.

He woke up suddenly in the broad daylight. The horse was listening to something, his head up. Swiftly, Ches went to the horse and led it back under the overhang. Then he drew on his boots, rolled his blankets, and saddled the horse. Still he heard no sound.

Climbing the rim again, he studied the desert and found nothing. Returning to his horse, he mounted up and rode down the canyon toward the flatland beyond. Coming out of the canyon mouth, he rode right into the middle of a war party of more than twenty Apaches—invisible until suddenly they stood up behind rocks, their rifles leveled. And he didn't have a chance.

Swiftly, they bound his wrists to the saddle horn and tied his feet. Only then did he see the man who led the party. It was Cochise.

He was a lean, wiry Indian of past fifty, his black hair streaked with gray, his features strong and clean-cut. He stared at Lane, and there was nothing in his face to reveal what he might be thinking.

Several of the younger warriors pushed forward, talking excitedly and waving their arms. Ches Lane understood some of it, but he sat straight in the saddle, his head up, waiting. Then Cochise spoke and the party turned, and, leading his horse, they rode away.

The miles grew long and the sun was hot. He was offered no water and he asked for none. The Indians ignored him. Once a young brave rode near and struck him viciously. Lane made no sound, gave no indication of pain. When they finally stopped, it was beside a huge anthill swarming with big red desert ants.

Roughly, they quickly untied him and jerked him from his horse. He dug in his heels and shouted at them in Spanish: "The Apaches are women! They tie me to the ants because they are afraid to fight me!"

An Indian struck him, and Ches glared at the man. If he must die, he would show them how it should be done. Yet he knew the unpredictable nature of the Indian, of his great respect for courage.

"Give me a knife, and I'll kill any of your warriors!"

They stared at him, and one powerfully built Apache angrily ordered them to get on with it. Cochise spoke, and the big warrior replied angrily.

Ches Lane nodded at the anthill. "Is this the death for a fighting man? I have fought your strong men and beaten them. I have left no trail for them to follow, and for months I have lived among you, and now only by accident have you captured me. Give me a knife," he added grimly, "and I will fight him!" He indicated the big, black-faced Apache.

The warrior's cruel mouth hardened, and he struck Ches across the face.

The white man tasted blood and fury. "Woman!" Ches said. "Coyote! You are afraid!" Ches turned on Cochise, as the Indians stood irresolute. "Free my hands and let me fight!" he demanded. "If I win, let me go free."

Cochise said something to the big Indian. Instantly, there was stillness. Then an Apache sprang forward and, with a slash of his knife, freed Lane's hands. Shaking loose the thongs, Ches Lane chafed his wrists to bring back the circulation. An Indian threw a knife at his feet. It was his own bowie knife.

Ches took off his riding boots. In sock feet, his knife gripped low in his hand, its cutting edge up, he looked at the big warrior.

"I promise you nothing," Cochise said in Spanish, "but an honorable death."

The big warrior came at him on cat feet. Warily, Ches circled. He had not only to defeat this Apache but to escape. He permitted himself a side glance toward his horse. It stood alone. No Indian held it.

The Apache closed swiftly, thrusting wickedly with the knife. Ches, who had learned knife-fighting in the bayou country of Louisiana, turned his hip sharply, and the blade slid past him. He struck swiftly, but the Apache's forward movement deflected the blade, and it failed to penetrate. However, as it swept up between the Indian's body and arm, it cut a deep gash in the warrior's left armpit.

The Indian sprang again, like a clawing cat, streaming blood. Ches moved aside, but a backhand sweep nicked him, and he felt the sharp bite of the blade. Turning, he paused on the balls of his feet.

He had had no water in hours. His lips were cracked. Yet he sweated now, and the salt of it stung his eyes. He stared into the malevolent black eyes of the Apache, then moved to meet him. The Indian lunged, and Ches sidestepped like a boxer and spun on the ball of his foot.

The sudden side step threw the Indian past him, but Ches failed to drive the knife into the Apache's kidney when his foot rolled on a stone. The point left a thin red line across the Indian's back. The Indian was quick. Before Ches could recover his balance, he grasped the white man's knife wrist. Desperately, Ches grabbed for the Indian's knife hand and got the wrist, and they stood there straining, chest to chest.

Ches cut a deep gash in the warrior's left armpit.

Seeing his chance, Ches suddenly let his knees buckle, then brought up his knee and fell back, throwing the Apache over his head to the sand. Instantly, he whirled and was on his feet, standing over the Apache. The warrior had lost his knife, and he lay there, staring up, his eyes black with hatred.

Coolly, Ches stepped back, picked up the Indian's knife, and tossed it to him contemptuously. There was a grunt from the watching Indians, and then his antagonist rushed. But loss of blood had weakened the warrior, and Ches stepped in swiftly, struck the blade aside, then thrust the point of his blade hard against the Indian's belly.

Black eyes glared into his without yielding. A thrust, and the man would be disemboweled, but Ches stepped back. "He is a strong man," Ches said in Spanish. "It is enough that I have won."

Deliberately, he walked to his horse and swung into the saddle. He looked around, and every rifle covered him.

So he had gained nothing. He had hoped that mercy might lead to mercy, that the Apache's respect for a fighting man would win his freedom. He had failed. Again they bound him to his horse, but they did not take his knife from him.

When they camped at last, he was given food and drink. He was bound again, and a blanket was thrown over him. At daylight they were again in the saddle. In Spanish he asked where they were taking him, but they gave no indication of hearing. When they stopped again, it was beside a pole corral, near a stone cabin.

———

When Jimmy spoke, Angie got quickly to her feet. She recognized Cochise with a start of relief, but she saw instantly that this was a war party. And then she saw the prisoner.

Their eyes met and she felt a distinct shock. He was a white man, a big, unshaven man who badly needed both a bath and a haircut, his clothes ragged and bloody. Cochise gestured at the prisoner.

"No take Apache man, you take white man. This man good for hunt, good for fight. He strong warrior. You take 'em."

Flushed and startled, Angie stared at the prisoner and caught a faint glint of humor in his dark eyes.

"Is this here the fate worse than death I hear tell of?" he inquired gently.

"Who are you?" she asked, and was immediately conscious that it was an extremely silly question.

The Apaches had drawn back and were watching curiously. She could do nothing for the present but accept the situation. Obviously they intended to do her a kindness, and it would not do to offend them. If they had not brought this man to her, he might have been killed.

"Name's Ches Lane, ma'am," he said. "Will you untie me? I'd feel a lot safer."

"Of course." Still flustered, she went to him and untied his hands. One Indian said something, and the others chuckled; then, with a whoop, they swung their horses and galloped off down the canyon.

Their departure left her suddenly helpless, the shadowy globe of her loneliness shattered by this utterly strange man standing before her, this big, bearded man brought to her out of the desert.

She smoothed her apron, suddenly pale as she realized what his delivery to her implied. What must he think of her? She turned away quickly. "There's hot water," she said hastily, to prevent his speaking. "Dinner is almost ready."

She walked quickly into the house and stopped before the stove, her mind a blank. She looked around her as if she had suddenly waked up in a strange place. She heard water being poured into the basin by the door, and heard him take Ed's razor. She had never moved the box. To have moved it would—

"Sight of work done here, ma'am."

She hesitated, then turned with determination and stepped into the doorway. "Yes, Ed—"

"You're Angie Lowe."

Surprised, she turned toward him and recognized his own startled awareness of her. As he shaved, he told her about Ed, and what had happened that day in the saloon.

"He—Ed was like that. He never considered consequences until it was too late."

"Lucky for me he didn't."

He was younger looking with his beard gone. There was a certain quiet dignity in his face. She went back inside and began putting plates on the table. She was conscious that he had moved to the door and was watching her.

"You don't have to stay," she said. "You owe me nothing. Whatever Ed did, he did because he was that kind of person. You aren't responsible."

He did not answer, and when she turned again to the stove, she glanced swiftly at him. He was looking across the valley.

There was a studied deference about him when he moved to a place at the table. The children stared, wide-eyed and silent; it had been so long since a man sat at this table.

Angie could not remember when she had felt like this. She was awkwardly conscious of her hands, which never seemed to be in the right place or doing the right things. She scarcely tasted her food, nor did the children.

Ches Lane had no such inhibitions. For the first time, he realized how hungry he was. After the half-cooked meat of lonely, trailside fires, this was tender and flavored. Hot biscuits, desert honey . . . Suddenly he looked up, embarrassed at his appetite.

"You were really hungry," she said.

"Man can't fix much, out on the trail."

Later, after he'd got his bedroll from his saddle and unrolled it on the hay in the barn, he walked back to the house and sat on the lowest step. The sun was gone, and they watched the cliffs stretch their red shadows across the valley. A quail called plaintively, a mellow sound of twilight.

"You needn't worry about Cochise," she said. "He'll soon be crossing into Mexico."

"I wasn't thinking about Cochise."

That left her with nothing to say, and she listened again to the quail and watched a lone bright star in the sky.

"A man could get to like it here," he said quietly.

The Blood Bay

By Annie Proulx

THE WINTER OF 1886–87 was terrible. Every goddamn history of the high plains says so. There were great stocks of cattle on overgrazed land during the droughty summer. Early wet snow froze hard so the cattle could not break through the crust to the grass. Blizzards and freeze-eye cold followed, the gaunt bodies of cattle piling up in draws and coulees.

A young Montana cowboy, somewhat vain, had skimped on coat and mittens and put all his wages into a fine pair of handmade boots. He crossed into Wyoming Territory thinking it would be warmer, for it was south of where he was. That night he froze to death on Powder River's bitter west bank, that stream of famous dimensions and direction—an inch deep, a mile wide, and she flows uphill from Texas.

The next afternoon three cowpunchers from the Box Spring outfit near Suggs rode past his corpse, blue as a whetstone and half-buried in snow. They were savvy and salty. They wore blanket coats, woolly chaps, grease-wool scarves tied over their hats and under their bristled chins, sheepskin mitts, and two of them were fortunate enough to park their feet in good boots and heavy socks. The third, Dirt Sheets, a cross-eyed drinker of hair-oil, was all right on top but his luck was running muddy near the bottom, no socks and curl-toe boots cracked and holed.

"That can a corn beef's wearin' my size boots," Sheets said and got off his horse for the first time that day. He pulled at the Montana cowboy's left boot but it was frozen on. The right one didn't come off any easier.

"Son of a sick steer in a snowbank," he said, "I'll cut 'em off and thaw 'em after supper." Sheets pulled out a Bowie knife and sawed through Montana's shins just above the boot tops, put the booted feet in his saddlebags, admiring the tooled leather and topstitched hearts and clubs. They rode on down the river looking for strays, found a dozen bogged in deep drifts, and lost most of the daylight getting them out.

"Too late to try for the bunkhouse. Old man Grice's shack is somewheres up along. He's bound a have dried prunes or other dainties or at least a hot stove." The temperature was dropping, so cold that spit crackled in the air and a man didn't dare to piss for fear he'd be rooted fast until spring. They agreed it must be forty below and more, the wind scything up a nice Wyoming howler.

They found the shack four miles north. Old man Grice opened the door a crack.

"Come on in, puncher or rustler, I don't care."

"We'll put our horses up. Where's the barn."

"Barn. Never had one. There's a lean-to out there behind the woodpile should keep 'em from blowing away or maybe freezin'. I got my two horses in here beside the dish cupboard. I pamper them babies something terrible. Sleep where you can find a space, but I'm telling you don't bother that blood bay none, he will mull you up and spit you out. He's a spirited steed. Pull up a chair and have some a this son-of-a-bitch stew. And I got plenty conversation juice a wash it down. Hot biscuits just comin' out a the oven."

It was a fine evening, eating, drinking, and playing cards, swapping lies, the stove kicking out heat, old man Grice's spoiled horses sighing in comfort. The only disagreeable tone to the evening from the waddies' point of view was the fact that their host cleaned them out, took them for three dollars and four bits. Around midnight Grice blew out the lamp and got in his bunk, and the three punchers stretched out on the floor. Sheets set his trophies behind the stove, laid his head on his saddle, and went to sleep.

He woke half an hour before daylight, recalled it was his mother's birthday, and if he wanted to telegraph a filial sentiment to her, he would have to ride faster than chain lightning with the links snapped, for the Overland office closed at noon. He checked his grisly trophies, found them thawed and pulled

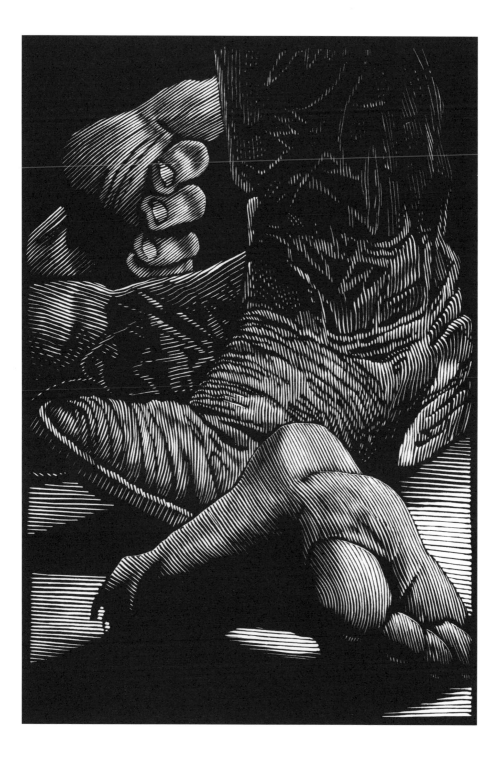

The bare Montana feet and his old boots.

the boots and socks off the originals, drew them onto his own pedal extremities. He threw the bare Montana feet and his old boots in the corner near the dish cupboard, slipped out like a falling feather, saddled his horse, and rode away. The wind was low and the fine cold air refreshed him.

Old man Grice was up with the sun grinding coffee beans and frying bacon. He glanced down at his rolled-up guests and said, "Coffee's ready." The blood bay stamped and kicked at something that looked like a man's foot. Old man Grice took a closer look.

"There's a bad start to the day," he said, "it is a man's foot and there's the other." He counted the sleeping guests. There were only two of them.

"Wake up, survivors, for god's sake wake up and get up."

The two punchers rolled out, stared wild-eyed at the old man who was fairly frothing, pointing at the feet on the floor behind the blood bay.

"He's ate Sheets. Ah, I knew he was a hard horse, but to eat a man whole. You savage bugger," he screamed at the blood bay and drove him out into the scorching cold. "You'll never eat human meat again. You'll sleep out with the blizzards and wolves, you hell-bound fiend." Secretly he was pleased to own a horse with the sand to eat a raw cowboy.

The leftover Box Spring riders were up and drinking coffee. They squinted at old man Grice, hitched at their gun belts.

"Ah, boys, for god's sake, it was a terrible accident. I didn't know what a brute of a animal was that blood bay. Let's keep this to ourselves. Sheets was no prize, and I've got forty gold dollars says so and the three and four bits I took off a you last night. Eat your bacon, don't make no trouble. There's enough trouble in the world without no more."

No, they wouldn't make trouble and they put the heavy money in their saddlebags, drank a last cup of hot coffee, saddled up, and rode out into the grinning morning.

When they saw Sheets that night at the bunkhouse, they nodded, congratulated him on his mother's birthday, but said nothing about blood bays or forty-three dollars and four bits. The arithmetic stood comfortable.

Three-Ten to Yuma

BY ELMORE LEONARD

HE HAD PICKED UP his prisoner at Fort Huachuca shortly after midnight and now, in a silent early morning mist, they approached Contention. The two riders moved slowly, one behind the other.

Entering Stockman Street, Paul Scallen glanced back at the open country with the wet haze blanketing its flatness, thinking of the long night ride from Huachuca, relieved that this much was over. When his body turned again, his hand moved over the sawed-off shotgun that was across his lap and he kept his eyes on the man ahead of him until they were near the end of the second block, opposite the side entrance of the Republic Hotel.

He said just above a whisper, though it was clear in the silence, "End of the line."

The man turned in his saddle, looking at Scallen curiously. "The jail's around on Commercial."

"I want you to be comfortable."

Scallen stepped out of the saddle, lifting a Winchester from the boot, and walked toward the hotel's side door. A figure stood in the gloom of the doorway, behind the screen, and as Scallen reached the steps the screen door opened.

"Are you the marshal?"

"Yes, sir." Scallen's voice was soft and without emotion. "Deputy, from Bisbee."

"We're ready for you. Two-oh-seven. A corner . . . fronts on Commercial." He sounded proud of the accommodation.

"You're Mr. Timpey?"

The man in the doorway looked surprised. "Yeah, Wells Fargo. Who'd you expect?"

"You might have got a back room, Mr. Timpey. One with no windows." He swung the shotgun on the man still mounted. "Step down easy, Jim."

The man, who was in his early twenties, a few years younger than Scallen, sat with one hand over the other on the saddle horn. Now he gripped the horn and swung down. When he was on the ground his hands were still close together, iron manacles holding them three chain lengths apart. Scallen motioned him toward the door with the stubby barrel of the shotgun.

"Anyone in the lobby?"

"The desk clerk," Timpey answered him, "and a man in a chair by the front door."

"Who is he?"

"I don't know. He's asleep . . . got his brim down over his eyes."

"Did you see anyone out on Commercial?"

"No . . . I haven't been out there." At first he had seemed nervous, but now he was irritated, and a frown made his face pout childishly.

Scallen said calmly, "Mr. Timpey, it was your line this man robbed. You want to see him go all the way to Yuma, don't you?"

"Certainly I do." His eyes went to the outlaw, Jim Kidd, then back to Scallen hurriedly. "But why all the melodrama? The man's under arrest—already been sentenced."

"But he's not in jail till he walks through the gates at Yuma," Scallen said. "I'm only one man, Mr. Timpey, and I've got to get him there."

"Well, dammit . . . I'm not the law! Why didn't you bring men with you? All I know is I got a wire from our Bisbee office to get a hotel room and meet you here the morning of November third. There weren't any instructions that I had to get myself deputized a marshal. That's your job."

"I know it is, Mr. Timpey," Scallen said, and smiled, though it was an effort. "But I want to make sure no one knows Jim Kidd's in Contention until after train time this afternoon."

Jim Kidd had been looking from one to the other with a faintly amused grin. Now he said to Timpey, "He means he's afraid somebody's going to jump him." He smiled at Scallen. "That marshal must've really sold you a bill of goods."

"What's he talking about?" Timpey said.

Kidd went on before Scallen could answer. "They hid me in the Huachuca lockup 'cause they knew nobody could get at me there . . . and finally the

Bisbee marshal gets a plan. He and some others hopped the train in Benson last night, heading for Yuma with an army prisoner passed off as me." Kidd laughed, as if the idea were ridiculous.

"Is that right?" Timpey said.

Scallen nodded. "Pretty much right."

"How does he know all about it?"

"He's got ears and ten fingers to add with."

"I don't like it. Why just one man?"

"Every deputy from here down to Bisbee is out trying to scare up the rest of them. Jim here's the only one we caught," Scallen explained—then added, "Alive."

Timpey shot a glance at the outlaw. "Is he the one who killed Dick Moons?"

"One of the passengers swears he saw who did it . . . and he didn't identify Kidd at the trial."

Timpey shook his head. "Dick drove for us a long time. You know his brother lives here in Contention. When he heard about it he almost went crazy." He hesitated, and then said again, "I don't like it."

Scallen felt his patience wearing away, but he kept his voice even when he said, "Maybe I don't either . . . but what you like and what I like aren't going to matter a whole lot, with the marshal past Tucson by now. You can grumble about it all you want, Mr. Timpey, as long as you keep it under your breath. Jim's got friends . . . and since I have to haul him clear across the territory, I'd just as soon they didn't know about it."

Timpey fidgeted nervously. "I don't see why I have to get dragged into this. My job's got nothing to do with law enforcement. . . ."

"You have the room key?"

"In the door. All I'm responsible for is the stage run between here and Tucson—"

Scallen shoved the Winchester at him. "If you'll take care of this and the horses till I get back, I'll be obliged to you . . . and I know I don't have to ask you not to mention we're at the hotel."

He waved the shotgun and nodded and Jim Kidd went ahead of him through the side door into the hotel lobby. Scallen was a stride behind him, holding the stubby shotgun close to his leg. "Up the stairs on the right, Jim."

Kidd started up, but Scallen paused to glance at the figure in the armchair near the front. He was sitting on his spine with limp hands folded on his stomach and, as Timpey had described, his hat low over the upper part of his face. You've seen people sleeping in hotel lobbies before, Scallen told himself, and followed Kidd up the stairs. He couldn't stand and wonder about it.

Room 207 was narrow and high-ceilinged, with a single window looking down on Commercial Street. An iron bed was placed the long way against one wall and extended to the right side of the window, and along the opposite wall was a dresser with washbasin and pitcher and next to it a rough-board wardrobe. An unpainted table and two straight chairs took up most of the remaining space.

"Lay down on the bed if you want to," Scallen said.

"Why don't you sleep?" Kidd asked. "I'll hold the shotgun."

The deputy moved one of the straight chairs near to the door and the other to the side of the table opposite the bed. Then he sat down, resting the shotgun on the table so that it pointed directly at Jim Kidd sitting on the edge of the bed near the window.

He gazed vacantly outside. A patch of dismal sky showed above the frame buildings across the way, but he was not sitting close enough to look directly down onto the street. He said, indifferently, "I think it's going to rain."

There was a silence, and then Scallen said, "Jim, I don't have anything against you personally . . . this is what I get paid for, but I just want it understood that if you start across the seven feet between us, I'm going to pull both triggers at once—without first asking you to stop. That clear?"

Kidd looked at the deputy marshal, then his eyes drifted out the window again. "It's kinda cold too." He rubbed his hands together and the three chain links rattled against each other. "The window's open a crack. Can I close it?"

Scallen's grip tightened on the shotgun and he brought the barrel up, though he wasn't aware of it. "If you can reach it from where you're sitting."

Kidd looked at the windowsill and said without reaching toward it, "Too far."

"All right," Scallen said, rising. "Lay back on the bed." He worked his gun belt around so that now the Colt was on his left hip.

Kidd went back slowly, smiling. "You don't take any chances, do you? Where's your sporting blood?"

"Down in Bisbee with my wife and three youngsters," Scallen told him without smiling, and moved around the table.

There were no grips on the window frame. Standing with his side to the window, facing the man on the bed, he put the heel of his hand on the bottom ledge of the frame and shoved down hard. The window banged shut and with the slam he saw Jim Kidd kicking up off of his back, his body straining to rise without his hands to help. Momentarily, Scallen hesitated and his finger tensed on the trigger. Kidd's feet were on the floor, his body swinging up and his head down to lunge from the bed. Scallen took one step and brought his knee up hard against Kidd's face.

The outlaw went back across the bed, his head striking the wall. He lay there with his eyes open looking at Scallen.

"Feel better now, Jim?"

Kidd brought his hands up to his mouth, working the jaw around. "Well, I had to try you out," he said. "I didn't think you'd shoot."

"But you know I will the next time."

For a few minutes Kidd remained motionless. Then he began to pull himself straight. "I just want to sit up."

Behind the table Scallen said, "Help yourself." He watched Kidd stare out the window.

Then, "How much do you make, Marshal?" Kidd asked the question abruptly.

"I don't think it's any of your business."

"What difference does it make?"

Scallen hesitated. "A hundred and fifty a month," he said, finally, "some expenses, and a dollar bounty for every arrest against a Bisbee ordinance in the town limits."

Kidd shook his head sympathetically. "And you got a wife and three kids."

"Well, it's more than a cowhand makes."

"But you're not a cowhand."

"I've worked my share of beef."

"Forty a month and keep, huh?" Kidd laughed.

"That's right, forty a month," Scallen said. He felt awkward. "How much do you make?"

Kidd grinned. When he smiled he looked very young, hardly out of his teens. "Name a month," he said. "It varies."

"But you've made a lot of money."

"Enough. I can buy what I want."

"What are you going to be wanting the next five years?"

"You're pretty sure we're going to Yuma."

"And you're pretty sure we're not," Scallen said. "Well, I've got two train passes and a shotgun that says we are. What've you got?"

Kidd smiled. "You'll see." Then he said right after it, his tone changing, "What made you join the law?"

"The money," Scallen answered, and felt foolish as he said it. But he went on, "I was working for a spread over by the Pantano Wash when Old Nana broke loose and raised hell up the Santa Rosa Valley. The army was going around in circles, so the Pima County marshal got up a bunch to help out and we tracked Apaches almost all spring. The marshal and I got along fine, so he offered me a deputy job if I wanted it." He wanted to say that he started for seventy-five and worked up to the one hundred and fifty, but he didn't.

"And then someday you'll get to be marshal and make two hundred."

"Maybe."

"And then one night a drunk cowhand you've never seen will be tearing up somebody's saloon and you'll go in to arrest him and he'll drill you with a lucky shot before you get your gun out."

"So you're telling me I'm crazy."

"If you don't already know it."

Scallen took his hand off the shotgun and pulled tobacco and paper from his shirt pocket and began rolling a cigarette. "Have you figured out yet what my price is?"

Kidd looked startled, momentarily, but the grin returned. "No, I haven't. Maybe you come higher than I thought."

Scallen scratched a match across the table, lighted the cigarette, then threw it to the floor, between Kidd's boots. "You don't have enough money, Jim."

Kidd shrugged, then reached down for the cigarette. "You've treated me pretty good. I just wanted to make it easy on you."

The sun came into the room after a while. Weakly at first, cold and hazy. Then it warmed and brightened and cast an oblong patch of light between the bed and the table. The morning wore on slowly because there was nothing to do and each man sat restlessly thinking about somewhere else, though it was a restlessness within and it showed on neither of them.

The deputy rolled cigarettes for the outlaw and himself and most of the time they smoked in silence. Once Kidd asked him what time the train left. He told him shortly after three, but Kidd made no comment.

Scallen went to the window and looked out at the narrow rutted road that was Commercial Street. He pulled a watch from his vest pocket and looked at it. It was almost noon, yet there were few people about. He wondered about this and asked himself if it was unnaturally quiet for a Saturday noon in Contention . . . or if it were just his nerves. . . .

He studied the man standing under the wooden awning across the street, leaning idly against a support post with his thumbs hooked in his belt and his flat-crowned hat on the back of his head. There was something familiar about him. And each time Scallen had gone to the window—a few times during the past hour—the man had been there.

He glanced at Jim Kidd lying across the bed, then looked out the window in time to see another man moving up next to the one at the post. They stood together for the space of a minute before the second man turned a horse from the tie rail, swung up, and rode off down the street.

The man at the post watched him go and tilted his hat against the sun glare. And then it registered. With the hat low on his forehead Scallen saw him again as he had that morning. The man lying in the armchair . . . as if asleep.

He saw his wife, then, and the three youngsters and he could almost feel the little girl sitting on his lap where she had climbed up to kiss him good-bye, and he had promised to bring her something from Tucson. He didn't know why they had come to him all of a sudden. And after he had put them out of his mind, since there was no room now, there was an upset feeling inside as if he had swallowed something that would not go down all the way. It made his heart beat a little faster.

Jim Kidd was smiling up at him. "Anybody I know?"

"I didn't think it showed."

"Like the sun going down."

Scallen glanced at the man across the street and then to Jim Kidd. "Come here." He nodded to the window. "Tell me who your friend is over there."

Kidd half rose and leaned over looking out the window, then sat down again. "Charlie Prince."

"Somebody else just went for help."

"Charlie doesn't need help."

"How did you know you were going to be in Contention?"

You told that Wells Fargo man I had friends . . . and about the posses chasing around in the hills. Figure it out for yourself. You could be looking out a window in Benson and seeing the same thing."

"They're not going to do you any good."

"I don't know any man who'd get himself killed for a hundred and fifty dollars." Kidd paused. "Especially a man with a wife and young ones. . . ."

Men rode to town in something less than an hour later. Scallen heard the horses coming up Commercial, and went to the window to see the six riders pull to a stop and range themselves in a line in the middle of the street facing the hotel. Charlie Prince stood behind them, leaning against the post.

Then he moved away from it, leisurely, and stepped down into the street. He walked between the horses and stopped in front of them just below the window. He cupped his hands to his mouth and shouted, "Jim!"

In the quiet street it was like a pistol shot.

Scallen looked at Kidd, seeing the smile that softened his face and was even in his eyes. Confidence. It was all over him. And even with the manacles on, you would believe that it was Jim Kidd who was holding the shotgun.

"What do you want me to tell him?" Kidd said.

"Tell him you'll write every day."

Kidd laughed and went to the window, pushing it up by the top of the frame. It raised a few inches. Then he moved his hands under the window and it slid up all the way.

"Charlie, you go buy the boys a drink. We'll be down shortly."

"Are you all right?"

"Sure I'm all right."

Charlie Prince hesitated. "What if you don't come down? He could kill you and say you tried to break. . . . Jim, you tell him what'll happen if we hear a gun go off."

"He knows," Kidd said, and closed the window. He looked at Scallen standing motionless with the shotgun under his arm. "Your turn, Marshal."

"What do you expect me to say?"

"Something that makes sense. You said before I didn't mean a thing to you personally—what you're doing is just a job. Well, you figure out if it's worth getting killed for. All you have to do is throw your guns on the bed and let me walk out the door and you can go back to Bisbee and arrest all the drunks you want. Nobody's going to blame you with the odds stacked seven to one. You know your wife's not going to complain. . . ."

"You should have been a lawyer, Jim."

The smile began to fade from Kidd's face. "Come on—what's it going to be?"

The door rattled with three knocks in quick succession. Abruptly the room was silent. The two men looked at each other and now the smile disappeared from Kidd's face completely.

Scallen moved to the side of the door, tiptoeing in his high-heeled boots, then pointed his shotgun toward the bed. Kidd sat down.

"Who is it?"

For a moment there was no answer. Then he heard, "Timpey."

He glanced at Kidd, who was watching him. "What do you want?"

"I've got a pot of coffee for you."

Scallen hesitated. "You alone?"

"Of course I am. Hurry up, it's hot!"

He drew the key from his coat pocket, then held the shotgun in the crook of his arm as he inserted the key with one hand and turned the knob with the other. The door opened—and slammed against him, knocking him back against the dresser. He went off balance, sliding into the wardrobe, going down on his hands and knees, and the shotgun clattered across the floor to the window. He saw Jim Kidd drop to the floor for the gun. . . .

"Hold it!"

A heavyset man stood in the doorway with a Colt pointing out past the thick bulge of his stomach. "Leave that shotgun where it is." Timpey stood next to him with the coffeepot in his hand. There was coffee down the front of his suit, on the door, and on the flooring. He brushed at the front of his coat feebly, looking from Scallen to the man with the pistol.

"I couldn't help it, Marshal—he made me do it. He threatened to do something to me if I didn't."

"Who is he?"

"Bob Moons . . . you know, Dick's brother. . . ."

The heavyset man glanced at Timpey angrily. "Shut your damn whining." His eyes went to Jim Kidd and held there. "You know who I am, don't you?"

Kidd looked uninterested. "You don't resemble anybody I know."

"You didn't have to know Dick to shoot him!"

"I didn't shoot that messenger."

Scallen got to his feet, looking at Timpey. "What the hell's wrong with you?"

"I couldn't help it. He forced me."

"How did he know we were here?"

"He came in this morning talking about Dick and I felt he needed some cheering up, so I told him Jim Kidd had been tried and was being taken to Yuma and was here in town . . . on his way. Bob didn't say anything and went out, and a little later he came back with the gun."

"You damn fool." Scallen shook his head wearily.

"Never mind all the talk." Moons kept the pistol on Kidd. "I would've found him sooner or later. This way everybody gets saved a long train ride."

"You pull that trigger," Scallen said, "and you'll hang for murder."

"Like he did for killing Dick. . . ."

"A jury said he didn't do it." Scallen took a step toward the big man. "And I'm damned if I'm going to let you pass another sentence."

"You stay put or I'll pass sentence on you!"

Scallen moved a slow step nearer. "Hand me the gun, Bob."

"I'm warning you—get the hell out of the way and let me do what I came for."

"Bob, hand me the gun or I swear I'll beat you through that wall."

Scallen tensed to take another step, another slow one. He saw Moons's eyes dart from him to Kidd and in that instant he knew it would be his only chance. He lunged, swinging his coat aside with his hand, and when the hand came up it was holding a Colt. All in one motion. The pistol went up and chopped an arc across Moons's head before the big man could bring his own gun around. His hat flew off as the barrel swiped his skull and he went back against the wall heavily, then sank to the floor.

Scallen wheeled to face the window, thumbing the hammer back. But Kidd was still sitting on the edge of the bed with the shotgun at his feet.

The deputy relaxed, letting the hammer ease down. "You might have made it, that time."

Kidd shook his head. "I wouldn't have got off the bed." There was a note of surprise in his voice. "You know, you're pretty good. . . ."

At two-fifteen Scallen looked at his watch, then stood up, pushing the chair back. The shotgun was under his arm. In less than an hour they would leave the hotel, walk over Commercial to Stockman, and then up Stockman to the station. Three blocks. He wanted to go all the way. He wanted to get Jim Kidd on that train . . . but he was afraid.

He was afraid of what he might do once they were on the street. Even now his breath was short and occasionally he would inhale and let the air out slowly to calm himself. And he kept asking himself if it was worth it.

People would be in the windows and the doors, though you wouldn't see them. They'd have their own feelings and most of their hearts would be pounding . . . and they'd edge back of the door frames a little more. The man out on the street was something without a human nature or a personality of its own. He was on a stage. The street was another world.

Timpey sat on the chair in front of the door and, next to him, squatting on the floor with his back against the wall, was Moons. Scallen had unloaded Moons's pistol and placed it in the pitcher behind him. Kidd was on the bed.

Most of the time he stared at Scallen. His face bore a puzzled expression, making his eyes frown, and sometimes he would cock his head as if studying the deputy from a different angle.

Scallen stepped to the window now. Charlie Prince and another man were under the awning. The others were not in sight.

"You haven't changed you mind?" Kidd asked him seriously.

Scallen shook his head.

"I don't understand you. You risk your neck to save my life, now you'll risk it again to send me to prison."

Scallen looked at Kidd and suddenly felt closer to him than any man he knew. "Don't ask me, Jim," he said, and sat down again.

After that he looked at his watch every few minutes.

At five minutes to three he walked to the door, motioning Timpey aside, and turned the key in the lock. "Let's go, Jim." When Kidd was next to him he prodded Moons with the gun barrel. "Over on the bed. Mister, if I see or hear about

The others were not in sight.

you on the street before train time, you'll face an attempted murder charge." He motioned Kidd past him, then stepped into the hall and locked the door.

They went down the stairs and crossed the lobby to the front door, Scallen a stride behind with the shotgun barrel almost touching Kidd's back. Passing through the doorway he said as calmly as he could, "Turn left on Stockman and keep walking. No matter what you hear, keep walking."

As they stepped out into Commercial, Scallen glanced at the ramada where Charlie Prince had been standing, but now the saloon porch was an empty shadow. Near the corner, two horses stood under a sign that said EAT in red letters; and on the other side of Stockman the signs continued, lining the rutted main street to make it seem narrower. And beneath the signs, in the shadows, nothing moved. There was a whisper of wind along the ramadas. It whipped sand specks from the street and rattled them against clapboard, and the sound was hollow and lifeless. Somewhere a screen door banged, far away.

They passed the café, turning onto Stockman. Ahead, the deserted street narrowed with distance to a dead end at the rail station—a single-story building standing by itself, low and sprawling, with most of the platform in shadow. The westbound was there, along the platform, but the engine and most of the cars were hidden by the station house. White steam lifted above the roof, to be lost in the sun's glare.

They were almost to the platform when Kidd said over his shoulder, "Run like hell while you're still able."

"Where are they?"

Kidd grinned, because he knew Scallen was afraid. "How should I know?"

"Tell them to come out in the open!"

"Tell them yourself."

"Dammit, *tell* them!" Scallen clenched his jaw and jabbed the short barrel into Kidd's back. "I'm not fooling. If they don't come out, I'll kill you!"

Kidd felt the gun barrel hard against his spine and suddenly he shouted, "Charlie!"

It echoed in the street, but after there was only the silence. Kidd's eyes darted over the shadowed porches. "Dammit, Charlie—hold on!"

Scallen prodded him up the warped plank steps to the shade of the platform and suddenly he could feel them near. "Tell him again!"

"Don't shoot, Charlie!" Kidd screamed the words.

From the other side of the station they heard the trainman's call trailing off, ". . . Gila Bend. Sentinel, Yuma!"

The whistle sounded loud, wailing, as they passed into the shade of the platform, then out again to the naked glare of the open side. Scallen squinted, glancing toward the station office, but the train dispatcher was not in sight. Nor was anyone. "It's the mail car," he said to Kidd. "The second to last one." Steam hissed from the iron cylinder of the engine, clouding that end of the platform. "Hurry it up!" he snapped, pushing Kidd along.

Then, from behind, hurried footsteps sounded on the planking, and, as the hiss of steam died away—"Stand where you are!"

The locomotive's main rods strained back, rising like the legs of a grotesque grasshopper, and the wheels moved. The connecting rods stopped on an upward swing and couplings clanged down the line of cars.

"Throw the gun away, brother!"

Charlie Prince stood at the corner of the station house with a pistol in each hand. Then he moved around carefully between the two men and the train. "Throw it far away, and unhitch your belt," he said.

"Do what he says," Kidd said. "They've got you."

The others, six of them, were strung out in the dimness of the platform shed. Grim faced, stubbles of beard, hat brims low. The man nearest Prince spat tobacco lazily.

Scallen knew fear at that moment as fear had never gripped him before; but he kept the shotgun hard against Kidd's spine. He said, just above a whisper, "Jim—I'll cut you in half!"

Kidd's body was stiff, his shoulders drawn up tightly. "Wait a minute. . . ." he said. He held his palms out to Charlie Prince, though he could have been speaking to Scallen.

Suddenly Prince shouted, "Go down!"

There was a fraction of a moment of dead silence that seemed longer. Kidd hesitated. Scallen was looking at the gunman over Kidd's shoulder, seeing the two pistols. Then Kidd was gone, rolling on the planking, and the pistols were coming up, one ahead of the other. Without moving, Scallen squeezed both triggers of the scattergun.

Charlie Prince was going down, holding his hands tight to his chest, as Scallen dropped the shotgun and swung around drawing his Colt. He fired hurriedly. *Wait for a target!* Words in his mind. He saw the men under the platform shed, three of them breaking for the station office, two going full length to the planks . . . one crouched, his pistol up. *That one! Get him quick!* Scallen aimed and squeezed the heavy revolver and the man went down. *Now get the hell out!*

Charlie Prince was facedown. Kidd was crawling, crawling frantically and coming to his feet when Scallen reached him. He grabbed Kidd by the collar savagely, pushing him on, and dug the pistol into his back. "Run, damn you!"

Gunfire erupted from the shed and thudded into the wooden caboose as they ran past it. The train was moving slowly. Just in front of them a bullet smashed a window of the mail car. Someone screamed, "You'll hit Jim!" There was another shot, then it was too late. Scallen and Kidd leapt up on the car platform and were in the mail car as it rumbled past the end of the station platform.

Kidd was on the floor, stretched out along a row of mail sacks. He rubbed his shoulder awkwardly with his manacled hands and watched Scallen, who stood against the wall next to the open door.

Kidd studied the deputy for some minutes. Finally he said, "You know, you really earn your hundred and a half."

From *The Secret Life of Cowboys*

BY TOM GRONEBERG

A PACK OF BARKING DOGS circles me. The front door opens before I get to it and a heavyset man in his middle forties, with a boyish face and a head of gray hair, shakes my hand and waves me inside, kicking at the dogs to keep them out. He nods at a woman who is busy washing dishes at the kitchen sink, and says, "That's Elsie." We sit on stools at a counter that separates the kitchen from the family room. The man, Calvin, tucks a pinch of Copenhagen in his lower lip and says, "Tell me about the horses."

I tell him the same story I have been telling myself. College boy turned wrangler turned college boy turned inside out. Unacademic jazz cipher meets Montana and falls in love. I want to reassure him that I am a good guy, that I won't rip him off. "I understand there is a lot of trust involved when you hire someone on," I say. "I know that you and your wife are taking a risk, letting a stranger into your lives."

Calvin looks over at Elsie and snorts, "She's my mother." I tell myself to keep my mouth shut. Calvin hires me nevertheless, saying, "Let's give it a try." He tells me that the ranch is 11,000 acres of deeded land plus another 18,000 acres leased from the Flathead Indian Reservation and the state of Montana. The ranch runs a thousand head of cattle. The calves are weaned in the fall and placed in feedlots, where they stay until the market is good enough, and then they're sold. Calvin says, "There's two other guys working here, Andy and Bert. Bert gets Saturdays off and you'll get Sundays. One more thing," he adds, putting a ratty plaid cap on his head and standing. "Don't use them as examples of how you should work."

Together we walk toward the barn. It is a low building made of rough-hewn wood with two doors, a large one and a smaller one, facing the house. As we go through the smaller door, I notice there is no horseshoe nailed above it, and I wonder why I expected to see one. The interior of the barn is gathered in shadows. The smell of hay and dirt and fresh manure remind me of the yeasty scent of dark imported beer. To the left there is a small tack room, home to a collection of dusty saddles and bridles and cats. Past the tack room, around the perimeter of the barn, are a dozen stalls built of rough two-by-eights. My eyes adjust to the darkness and I see a cow sleeping next to a large round hay bale in the middle of the barn. The bale is six feet tall, set on end like a barrel, and a pitchfork leans against it. Another cow stands by one of the far stalls, eating from a rubber feeder. A man sits on a stool, milking this cow. He looks to be in his fifties and has a wild beard and thick eyeglasses. The cow hits the man in his face with her tail as he pumps away at her udder.

"That's Andy," Calvin says, and we walk over. Andy fixes me with a look; his eyes, the color of glue, are magnified behind the lenses of his glasses. I nod dumbly as Calvin introduces us. Andy stands and I think he is going to shake my hand, but he takes the pail and walks around the barn, pouring milk into small dishes for the cats, which gather at his feet. Andy sets the bucket down, goes to a stall, and opens the gate. Two calves run out and start sucking greedily at the quarters of the cow's udder that Andy has left unmilked. I learn that these calves are bums, orphans.

Calvin jerks a thumb at the sleeping cow and says, "In nature, the animals take care of themselves first and abort the thing. But with cows, they give everything to the calf, even if it kills them." I see that the cow near the bale is not sleeping, she is dead. Her tail lies in a pile of afterbirth. Calvin is looking at the cow, mild disgust on his face. "I guess I better introduce you to Bert," he says. "You'll help him feed and then you guys can come back here and take care of this." I turn away from the dead cow and follow Calvin to the granary. This building is three stories high and built entirely of two-by-fours stacked on top of each other and spiked together. It is a tight building, constructed to keep the grain in and the mice and weather out. Calvin and I walk around the corner of the granary and find Bert leaning against a pickup truck, holding a steaming cup of coffee and a cigarette. Bert is in his sixties and is five and a half feet of salt and scabs. He doesn't even blink when he sees Calvin and me, doesn't even care that we caught him taking a break. I become his shadow.

We stack forty fifty-pound sacks of grain into the back of a wrecked ranch pickup, then load ourselves into the cab. The orange truck had been stripped of all knobs and mirrors and accessories. The passenger window is permanently down, the crank gone. Bert pulls into a feedlot and parks the truck between rows of long wooden feed troughs. There isn't much snow in the feedlots and the frost barely makes the muck stiff. The yearlings crowd around me, and hundreds of hooves suck in and out of the mud. I have never been this close to cattle before. I grab a sack of grain and struggle to a feed trough, trying not to fall down in the slop. I set the bag in the trough, untie the twine that holds it closed, then pour the grain along the length of the feeder. I work one row of feeders, Bert works the other. The yearlings crowd in closer, their pink curling tongues working over the smooth wood of the troughs, licking up the grain. These animals are twelve months old and each weighs 800 pounds. I am afraid that the cattle are going to kick me or crush me or bite me, but they are too busy eating to even consider me.

Bert drives. I get the gates. We go from feedlot to lot, working around the buildings. In one pen, a mottled steer stands in front of the pickup and will not move. Bert punches the horn, but like nearly everything else on the truck, it is broken.

After we have fed our way through the lots around the ranch headquarters, we drive to a distant feedlot across an earthen dike. There is a reservoir on one side of the narrow road and a thirty-foot dropoff on the other. Bert tells me, "The last kid we had working here drove into the pond his first time across. Next day, he drove off the other side and wrecked the truck." Bert says, "If it's muddy, stay in the ruts. If it's dry, straddle them, to keep from getting the truck high-centered." I'm starting to think I should have brought a notebook.

We make it across the dike and pull into the large feedlot, which is tucked against a hillside. There is another barn here and a set of corrals. A herd of horses stands in a nearby pasture. The feeder cattle converge on the truck. Bert clacks his false teeth and says, "Piranhas." We empty the last bags of grain, then Bert drives around to the hay bunks. There are fifteen half-ton hay bales lined up along a wooden fence. Bert starts at one end with a pitchfork, and I start at the other. We flake hay from the bales up against the rails of the feeder so that

A steer stood in front of the pickup and would not move.

the cattle can stick their heads through and eat it. It takes half an hour to get this done. My arms ache, but the pain is honest. It feels good.

We walk over to the second barn, where seventy brood mares cluster around another set of feeders. "These are just for breeding," Bert says. A half-dozen colts in a nearby pen eat hay from a round bale feeder. Bert and I move these young horses to another corral away from the feeder and then let the stud horse loose from a barn stall. He is a sorrel stallion, shaggy with his winter coat. The stud horse trots down the alleyway into the pen and begins eating hay. "Lucky bastard," Bert says as he closes the gate.

We are done feeding. To keep the empty grain bags from blowing out of the truck bed, Bert weighs them down with a handyman jack. We drive back across the dike to the main barn.

—

We eat in the bunkhouse, where Andy lives. The log building is the size of a classroom. The front part holds a couch and a recliner on a bare plywood floor. Off to the side there is a small abandoned kitchen. I sit on one end of the couch, next to Bert, who drinks coffee from a Thermos. Andy sits across from us in the recliner, near the woodstove. I never thought to bring a lunch. Bert offers me half of his venison sandwich, but I decline, not wanting to put him out. We sit with our work clothes on, jackets and boots and hats, everything but our gloves. The men eat without words.

Andy reaches into his cooler and takes out a bag of corn chips. He unrolls the bag, takes out a chip, pops it in his mouth, and rolls the bag closed again. Then he repeats the process. I want to know why Andy doesn't just leave the bag open, so I look over to Bert, but he is lost in his coffee. Andy sits, unfathomable, looking at me from behind his big glasses, eating his chips one by one. Then he is finished. He packs his pipe with tobacco from a tin of Half and Half, and it is time to go back to work.

Calvin has a cow penned alongside the barn. "Go to my truck," he tells me, "and get me some good twine." When I return, the cow is struggling in a corner of the pen. There is a rope around her neck and she is snubbed to a post. Bert holds the loose end of the rope from outside the pen. Andy stands, smoking his pipe. The cow dips and twists, anchored by the rope. Calvin takes the twine from me and ties some knots in it. Then he puts the twine around his waist and approaches the rear of the cow. He reaches up under the cow's tail and fastens the ends of the twine to something inside her. He leans back into the twine and two black legs emerge, then a tail. The cow is bawling now, going down on her front knees as much as the rope will allow. There is an urgency to Calvin's actions, his cap tilted on his head, sweat on his forehead. The calf slips from the cow and flops onto the ground in a pile of blood and afterbirth. Calvin reaches down, unties the twine, and clears mucus from the calf's mouth and nose. The thing looks around, dazed, amazed to find itself in this place. Calvin climbs out of the pen and asks, "Now what was wrong with that?"

I've never seen the birth of anything before, not puppies or kittens or goldfish. I don't have the words to answer him. I want to say "Miracle" or "Nativity" or some other word I do not yet know. I come out with, "Nothing. That was really something."

Calvin wipes his forehead with a gooey hand. "The calf was backwards," he says. "Nearly killed both of them." He motions for Bert to turn the rope loose, then says to Andy, "Make sure the calf sucks, and keep the cow in for a while to make sure she don't prolapse, then turn them out." Calvin ties the twine onto the top rail of the pen, looks at me, and says, "Bert, go show him how to grind the grain," and then he turns and walks to the house.

Bert fires up the little John Deere tractor and we drive it over to the granary, where he shows me how to hook the power takeoff shaft of the tractor to the driveline on the grinder. Barley from the storage area of the granary is dumped into the grinder by means of a giant auger. The ground barley fills a large hopper. My job is to hold an empty woven plastic sack under the hopper, open the chute until the grain reaches the top of the bag, tie it closed with a foot-long piece of twine, then stack the full bags on a pallet. I wear a dust mask against the grain particles that hang in the air. It is hard, repetitive work. I lose myself in the whine of the grinder, the hum of the tractor. Hours later, Bert emerges from the dust and gives me the sign for break time. It is the end of my first day, and the only muscle that is not sore is my heart.

Twelve O'Clock

By Stephen Crane

"Where were you at twelve o'clock, noon, on the 9th of June, 1875?"
—Question on intelligent cross-examination.

1

"Excuse me," said Ben Roddle with graphic gestures to a group of citizens in Nantucket's store. "Excuse *me*! When them fellers in leather pants an' six-shooters ride in, I go home an' set in th' cellar. That's what I do. When you see me pirooting through the streets at th' same time an' occasion as them punchers, you kin put me down fer bein' crazy. Excuse *me*!"

"Why, Ben," drawled old Nantucket, "you ain't never really seen 'em turned loose. Why, I kin remember—in th' old days—when—"

"Oh, damn yer old days!" retorted Roddle. Fixing Nantucket with the eye of scorn and contempt, he said, "I suppose you'll be sayin' in a minute that in th' old days you used to kill Injuns, won't you?"

There was some laughter, and Roddle was left free to expand his ideas on the periodic visits of cowboys to the town. "Mason Rickets, he had ten big punkins a-sittin' in front of his store, an' them fellers from the Upside-down-P ranch shot 'em—shot 'em all—an' Rickets lyin' on his belly in th' store a-callin' fer 'em to quit it. An' what did they do! Why, they *laughed* at 'im—just *laughed* at 'im! That don't do a town no good. Now, how would an eastern capiterlist"—(it was the town's humor to be always gassing of phantom investors who were likely to come any moment and pay a thousand prices for everything)—"how would an eastern capiterlist like that? Why, you couldn't see 'im fer th' dust on his trail. Then he'd tell all his friends: 'That there town may be all right, but ther's too much loose-handed shootin' fer my money.' An' he'd be right, too. Them rich fellers, they don't make no bad breaks with their money. They watch it all th' time b'cause they know blame well there ain't hardly room fer their feet fer th' pikers an' tinhorns an' thimble-riggers what are layin' fer 'em. I tell you, one puncher racin' his cow-pony hell-bent-fer-election down Main Street an' yellin' an' shootin', an' nothin' at all done about it, would scare away a whole herd of capiterlists. An' it ain't right. It oughter be stopped."

A pessimistic voice asked: "How you goin' to stop it, Ben?"

"Organize," replied Roddle pompously. "Organize. That's the only way to make these fellers lay down. I—"

From the street sounded a quick scudding of pony hooves, and a party of cowboys swept past the door. One man, however, was seen to draw rein and dismount. He came clanking into the store. "Mornin', gentlemen," he said civilly.

"Mornin'," they answered in subdued voices.

He stepped to the counter and said, "Give me a paper of fine cut, please." The group of citizens contemplated him in silence. He certainly did not look threatening. He appeared to be a young man of twenty-five years, with a tan from wind and sun, with a remarkably clear eye from perhaps a period of enforced temperance, a quiet young man who wanted to buy some tobacco. A six-shooter swung low on his hip, but at the moment it looked more decorative than warlike; it seemed merely a part of his odd gala dress— his sombrero with its band of rattlesnake-skin, his great flaming neckerchief, his belt of embroidered Mexican leather, his high-heeled boots, his huge spurs. And, above all, his hair had been watered and brushed until it lay as close to his head as the fur lays to a wet cat. Paying for his tobacco, he withdrew.

Ben Roddle resumed his harangue. "Well, there you are! Looks like a calm man now, but in less 'n half an hour he'll be as drunk as three bucks an' a squaw, an' then—excuse *me!*"

2

On this day the men of two outfits had come into town, but Ben Roddle's ominous words were not justified at once. The punchers spent most of the morning in an attack on whiskey which was too earnest to be noisy.

At five minutes of eleven, a tall, lank, brick-colored cowboy strode over to Placer's Hotel. Placer's Hotel was a notable place. It was the best hotel within two hundred miles. Its office was filled with armchairs and brown papier-mâché receptacles. At one end of the room was a wooden counter painted a bright pink, and on this morning a man was behind the counter writing in a ledger. He was the proprietor of the hotel, but his customary humor was so sullen that all strangers immediately wondered why in life he had chosen to play the part of mine host. Near his left hand, double doors opened into the dining room, which in warm weather was always kept darkened in order to discourage the flies, which was not compassed at all.

Placer, writing in his ledger, did not look up when the tall cowboy entered.

"Mornin', mister," said the latter. "I've come to see if you kin grubstake th' hull crowd of us fer dinner t'day."

Placer did not then raise his eyes, but with a certain churlishness, as if it annoyed him that his hotel was patronized, he asked: "How many?"

"Oh, about thirty," replied the cowboy. "An' we want th' best dinner you kin raise an' scrape. Everything th' best. We don't care what it costs s' long as we git a good square meal. We'll pay a dollar a head: by God, we will! We won't kick on nothin' in th' bill if you do it up fine. If you ain't got it in th' house, rustle th' hull town fer it. That's our gait. So you just tear loose, an' we'll—"

At this moment the machinery of a cuckoo clock on the wall began to whirr, little doors flew open, and a wooden bird appeared and cried, "Cuckoo!" And this was repeated until eleven o'clock had been announced, while the cowboy, stupefied, glassy-eyed, stood with his red throat gulping. At the end he wheeled upon Placer and demanded: *"What in hell is that?"*

Placer revealed by his manner that he had been asked this question too many times. "It's a clock," he answered shortly.

"I know it's a clock," gasped the cowboy; "but what *kind* of a clock?"

"A cuckoo clock. Can't you see?"

86 ❧ COWBOY STORIES

The cowboy, recovering his self-possession by a violent effort, suddenly went shouting into the street. "Boys! Say, boys! Come 'ere a minute!"

His comrades, comfortably inhabiting a nearby saloon, heard his stentorian calls, but they merely said to one another: "What's th' matter with Jake?—he's off his nut again."

But Jake burst in upon them with violence. "Boys," he yelled, "come over to th' hotel! They got a clock with a bird inside it, an' when it's eleven o'clock or anything like that, th' bird comes out an' says, 'Toot-toot, toot-toot!' that way, as many times as whatever time of day it is. It's immense! Come on over!"

The roars of laughter which greeted his proclamation were of two qualities; some men laughing because they knew all about cuckoo clocks, and other men laughing because they had concluded that the eccentric Jake had been victimized by some wise child of civilization.

Old Man Crumford, a venerable ruffian who probably had been born in a corral, was particularly offensive with his loud guffaws of contempt. "Bird a-comin' out of a clock an' a-tellin' ye th' time! Haw-haw-haw!" He swallowed his whiskey. "A bird! a-tellin' ye th' time! Haw-haw! Jake, you ben up agin some new drink. You ben drinkin' lonely an' got up agin some snake-medicine licker. A bird a-tellin' ye th' time! Haw-haw!"

The shrill voice of one of the younger cowboys piped from the background.

"Brace up, Jake. Don't let 'em laugh at ye. Bring 'em that salt codfish of yourn what kin pick out th' ace."

"Oh, he's only kiddin' us. Don't pay no 'tention to 'im. He thinks he's smart."

A cowboy whose mother had a cuckoo clock in her house in Philadelphia spoke with solemnity. "Jake's a liar. There's no such clock in the world. What? A bird inside a clock to tell the time? Change your drink, Jake."

Jake was furious, but his fury took a very icy form. He bent a withering glance upon the last speaker. "I don't mean a live bird," he said, with terrible dignity. "It's a wooden bird, an'—"

"A wooden bird!" shouted Old Man Crumford. "Wooden bird a-tellin' ye th' time! Haw-haw!"

But Jake still paid his frigid attention to the Philadelphian. "An' if yer sober enough to walk, it ain't such a blame long ways from here to th' hotel, an' I'll bet my pile agin yours if you only got two bits."

"I don't want your money, Jake," said the Philadelphian. "Somebody's been stringin' you—that's all. I wouldn't take your money." He cleverly appeared to pity the other's innocence.

"You couldn't git my money," cried Jake, in sudden hot anger. "You couldn't git it. Now—since yer so fresh—let's see how much you got." He clattered some large gold pieces noisily upon the bar.

The Philadelphian shrugged his shoulders and walked away. Jake was triumphant. "Any more bluffers 'round here?" he demanded. "Any more? Any more bluffers? Where's all these here hot sports? Let 'em step up. Here's my money—come an' git it."

But they had ended by being afraid. To some of them his tale was absurd, but still one must be circumspect when a man throws forty-five dollars in gold upon the bar and bids the world come and win it. The general feeling was expressed by Old Man Crumford, when with deference he asked: "Well, this here bird, Jake—what kinder lookin' bird is it?"

"It's a little brown thing," said Jake briefly. Apparently he almost disdained to answer.

"Well—how does it work?" asked the old man, meekly.

"Why in blazes don't you go an' look at it?" yelled Jake. "Want me to paint it in iles fer you? Go an' look!"

3

Placer was writing in his ledger. He heard a great trample of feet and clink of spurs on the porch, and there entered quietly the band of cowboys, some of them swaying a trifle, and these last being the most painfully decorous of all. Jake was in advance. He waved his hand toward the clock. "There she is," he said laconically. The cowboys drew up and stared. There was some giggling, but a serious voice said half-audibly, "I don't see no bird."

Jake politely addressed the landlord. "Mister, I've fetched these here friends of mine in here to see yer clock—"

Placer looked up suddenly. "Well, they can see it, can't they?" he asked in sarcasm. Jake, abashed, retreated to his fellows.

There was a period of silence. From time to time the men shifted their feet. Finally, Old Man Crumford leaned toward Jake, and in a penetrating whisper demanded, "Where's th' bird?" Some frolicsome spirits on the outskirts began to call "Bird! Bird!" as men at a political meeting call for a particular speaker.

Jake removed his big hat and nervously mopped his brow.

The young cowboy with the shrill voice again spoke from the skirts of the crowd. "Jake, is ther' sure 'nough a bird in that thing?"

"Yes. Didn't I tell you once?"

"Then," said the shrill-voiced man, in a tone of conviction, "it ain't a clock at all. It's a birdcage."

"I tell you it's a clock," cried the maddened Jake, but his retort could hardly be heard above the howls of glee and derision which greeted the words of him of the shrill voice.

Old Man Crumford was again rampant. "Wooden bird a-tellin' ye th' time! Haw-haw!"

Amid the confusion Jake went again to Placer. He spoke almost in supplication. "Say, mister, what time does this here thing go off ag'in?"

Placer lifted his head, looked at the clock, and said, "Noon."

There was a stir near the door, and Big Watson of the Square-X outfit, at this time very drunk indeed, came shouldering his way through the crowd and cursing everybody. The men gave him much room, for he was notorious as a quarrelsome person when drunk. He paused in front of Jake, and spoke as through a wet blanket. "What's all this——monkeyin' about?"

Jake was already wild at being made a butt for everybody, and he did not give backward. "None a' your damn business, Watson."

"Huh?" growled Watson, with the surprise of a challenged bull.

"I said," repeated Jake distinctly, "it's none a' your damn business."

Watson whipped his revolver half out of its holster. "I'll make it m' business, then, you—"

But Jake had backed a step away, and was holding his left-hand palm outward toward Watson, while in his right he held his six-shooter, its muzzle pointing at the floor. He was shouting in a frenzy, "No—don't you try it, Watson! Don't you dare try it, or, by Gawd, I'll kill you, sure—*sure!*"

He was aware of a torment of cries about him from fearful men; from men who protested, from men who cried out because they cried out. But he kept his eyes on Watson, and those two glared murder at each other, neither seeming to breathe, fixed like statues.

Placer stood behind the counter with an aimed revolver in each hand.

A loud new voice suddenly rang out: "Hol' on a minute!" All spectators who had not stampeded turned quickly, and saw Placer standing behind his bright pink counter, with an aimed revolver in each hand.

"Cheese it!" he said. "I won't have no fightin' here. If you want to fight, git out in the street."

Big Watson laughed, and, speeding up his six-shooter like a flash of blue light, he shot Placer through the throat—shot the man as he stood behind his absurd pink counter with his two aimed revolvers in his incompetent hands. With a yell of rage and despair, Jake smote Watson on the pate with his heavy weapon, and knocked him sprawling and bloody. Somewhere a woman shrieked like windy, midnight death. Placer fell behind the counter, and down upon him came his ledger and his inkstand, so that one could not have told blood from ink.

The cowboys did not seem to hear, see, nor feel, until they saw numbers of citizens with Winchesters running wildly upon them. Old Man Crumford threw high a passionate hand. "Don't shoot! We'll not fight ye for 'im."

Nevertheless two or three shots rang, and a cowboy who had been about to gallop off suddenly slumped over on his pony's neck, where he held for a moment like an old sack, and then slid to the ground, while his pony, with flapping rein, fled to the prairie.

"In God's name, don't shoot!" trumpeted Old Man Crumford. "We'll not fight ye fer 'im!"

"It's murder," bawled Ben Roddle.

In the chaotic street it seemed for a moment as if everybody would kill everybody. "Where's the man what done it?" These hot cries seemed to declare a war which would result in an absolute annihilation of one side. But the cowboys were singing out against it. They would fight for nothing—yes—they often fought for nothing—but they would not fight for this dark something.

At last, when a flimsy truce had been made between the inflamed men, all parties went to the hotel. Placer, in some dying whim, had made his way out from behind the pink counter, and, leaving a horrible trail, had traveled to the center of the room, where he had pitched headlong over the body of Big Watson.

The men lifted the corpse and laid it at the side.

"Who done it?" asked a white, stern man.

A cowboy pointed at Big Watson. "That's him," he said huskily.

There was a curious grim silence, and then suddenly, in the death chamber, there sounded the loud whirring of the clock's works, little doors flew open, a tiny wooden bird appeared and cried "Cuckoo"—twelve times.

From *Riders of the Purple Sage*

By Zane Grey

"Look! . . . Jane, them 'leadin' steers have bolted. They're drawin' the stragglers, an' that'll pull the whole herd."

Jane was not quick enough to catch the details called out by Lassiter, but she saw the line of cattle lengthening. Then, like a stream of white bees pouring from a huge swarm, the steers stretched out from the main body. In a few moments, with astonishing rapidity, the whole herd got into motion. A faint roar of trampling hooves came to Jane's ears and gradually swelled; low, rolling clouds of dust began to rise above the sage.

"It's a stampede, an' a hummer," said Lassiter.

"Oh, Lassiter! The herd's running with the valley! It leads into the canyon! There's a straight jump-off!"

"I reckon they'll run into it, too. But that's a good many miles yet. An', Jane, this valley swings round almost north before it goes east. That stampede will pass within a mile of us."

The long, white, bobbing line of steers streaked swiftly through the sage, and a funnel-shaped dust-cloud arose at a low angle. A dull rumbling filled Jane's ears.

"I'm thinkin' of millin' that herd," said Lassiter. His gray glance swept up the slope to the west. "There's some specks an' dust way off toward the village. Mebbe that's Judkins an' his boys. It ain't likely he'll get here in time to help. You'd better hold Black Star here on this high ridge." He ran to his horse and, throwing off saddlebags and tightening the cinches, he leaped astride and galloped straight down across the valley.

The dull rumble of thousands of hooves.

Jane went for Black Star and, leading him to the summit of the ridge, she mounted and faced the valley with excitement and expectancy. She had heard of milling stampeded cattle and knew it was a feat accomplished by only the most daring riders.

The white herd was now strung out in a line two miles long. The dull rumble of thousands of hooves deepened into continuous low thunder, and as the steers swept swiftly closer, the thunder became a heavy roll. Lassiter crossed in a few moments the level of the valley to the eastern rise of ground and there waited the coming of the herd. Presently, as the head of the white line reached a point opposite to where Jane stood, Lassiter spurred his black into a run.

Jane saw him take a position on the off side of the leaders of the stampede, and there he rode. It was like a race. They swept on down the valley, and when the end of the white line neared Lassiter's first stand, the head had begun to swing round to the west. It swung slowly and stubbornly, yet surely, and gradually assumed a long, beautiful curve of moving white. To Jane's amaze she saw the leaders swinging, turning till they headed back toward her and up the valley. Out to the right of these wild plunging steers ran Lassiter's black, and Jane's keen eye appreciated the fleet stride and sure-footedness of the blind horse. Then it seemed that the herd moved in a great curve, a huge half-moon with the points of head and tail almost opposite and a mile apart. But Lassiter relentlessly crowded the leaders, sheering them to the left, turning them little by little. And the dust-blinded wild followers plunged on madly in the tracks of their leaders. This ever-moving, ever-changing curve of steers rolled toward Jane and, when below her, scarce half a mile, it began to narrow and close into a circle. Lassiter had ridden parallel with her position, turned toward her, then aside, and now he was riding directly away from her, all the time pushing the head of that bobbing line inward.

It was then that Jane, suddenly understanding Lassiter's feat, stared and gasped at the riding of this intrepid man. His horse was fleet and tireless, but blind. He had pushed the leaders around and around till they were about to turn in on the inner side of the end of that line of steers. The leaders were already running in a circle; the end of the herd was still running almost straight. But soon they would be wheeling. Then, when Lassiter had the circle formed, how would he escape? With Jane Withersteen prayer was as ready as praise; and she prayed for this man's safety. A circle of dust began to collect. Dimly, as through a yellow veil, Jane saw Lassiter press the leaders inward to close the gap in the sage. She lost sight of him in the dust; again she thought she saw the black, riderless now, rear and drag himself and fall. Lassiter had been thrown—lost! Then he reappeared running out of the dust into the sage. He had escaped, and she breathed again.

Spellbound, Jane Withersteen watched this stupendous mill wheel of steers. Here was the milling of the herd. The white running circle closed in upon the open space of sage. And the dust circles closed above into a pall. The ground quaked and the incessant thunder of pounding hooves rolled on. Jane felt deafened, yet she thrilled to a new sound. As the circle of sage lessened the steers began to bawl, and when it closed entirely there came a great upheaval in the center, and a terrible thumping of heads and clicking of horns. Bawling, climbing, goring, the great mass of steers on the inside wrestled in a crashing din, heaved and groaned under the pressure. Then came a deadlock. The inner strife ceased, and the hideous roar and crash. Movement went on in the outer circle, and that, too, gradually stilled. The white herd had come to a stop, and the pall of yellow dust began to drift away on the wind.

Shallow Graves

By E. C. "Teddy Blue" Abbott

I WASN'T NINETEEN YEARS old when I come up the trail with the Olive herd, but don't let that fool you. I was a man in my own estimation and a man in fact. I was no kid with the outfit but a top cowhand, doing a top hand's work, and there is nothing so wonderful about that. All I'd ever thought about was being a good cowhand. I'd been listening to these Texas men and watching them and studying the disposition of cattle ever since I was eleven years old.

Even in years I was no younger than a lot of them. The average age of cowboys then, I suppose, was twenty-three or -four. Except for some of the bosses there was very few thirty-year-old men on the trail. I heard a story once about a schoolteacher who asked one of these old Texas cow dogs to tell her all about how he punched cows on the trail. She said: "Oh, Mister So-and-So, didn't the boys used to have a lot of fun riding their ponies?"

He said: "Madam, there wasn't any boys or ponies. They was all horses and men."

Well, they had to be, to stand the life they led. Look at the chances they took and the kind of riding they done, all the time, over rough country. Even in the daytime those deep coulees could open up all at once in front of you, before you had a chance to see where you were going, and at night it was something awful if you'd stop to think about it, which none of them ever did. If a storm come and the cattle started running—you'd hear that low rumbling noise along the ground and the men on herd wouldn't need to come in and tell you, you'd know—then you'd jump for your horse and get out there in the lead, trying to head them and get them into a mill before they scattered to hell and gone. It was riding at a dead run in the dark, with cut banks and prairie-dog holes all around you, not knowing if the next jump would land you in a shallow grave.

I helped to bury three of them in very shallow graves. The first one was after a run on the Blue River in '76. I was working for my father then, herding cattle outside Lincoln, and this outfit that had the run was part of a Texas trail herd belonging to John Lytle. He had sold five hundred cows to an Englishman named Jones—Lord Jones, they called him—on the Blue River. Three of Lytle's men were delivering the cows, and they took me along to help them because I knew the country, though I was only fifteen years old. We were camped close to Blue River one night, near a big prairie-dog town that was the furthest east of any prairie-dog town I ever saw—it's from there on to the Rockies that you strike them.

And that night it come up an awful storm. It took all four of us to hold the cattle and we didn't hold them, and when morning come there was one man missing. We went back to look for him, and we found him among the prairie-dog holes, beside his horse. The horse's ribs was scraped bare of hide, and all the rest of horse and man was mashed into the ground as flat as a pancake. The only thing you could recognize was the handle of his six-shooter. We tried to think the lightning hit him, and that was what we wrote his folks down in Henrietta, Texas. But we couldn't really believe it ourselves. I'm afraid it wasn't the lightning. I'm afraid his horse stepped into one of them holes and they both went down before the stampede.

We got a shovel—I remember it had a broken handle—and we buried him nearby, on a hillside covered with round, smooth rocks. We dug a little ground away underneath him and slipped his saddle blanket under him and piled the rocks on top. That was the best we could do. The ground was hard and we didn't have no proper tools.

But the awful part of it was that we had milled them cattle over him all night, not knowing he was there. That was what we couldn't get out of our minds. And after that, orders were given to sing when you were running with a stampede, so the others would know where you were as long as they heard you singing, and if they didn't hear you they would figure that something had

That was the best we could do.

happened. After awhile this grew to be a custom on the range, but you know this was still a new business in the seventies and they was learning all the time.

Coming up the trail in '81, we had a man killed in a big mix-up on the Washita, in the Nations, when six or seven herds was waiting for the river to go down, and a storm come and they all run together one night. And when I was coming up in '83, a man was killed in another outfit, going over a cut bank in broad daylight. His name was Davis, and he had a nickname I couldn't even tell you. He was with a roundup outfit on the French Fork of Republican River, right where the trail crosses it. We pulled in to water at noon, and we could see the roundup working further up the creek. It seems that two of them were trying to rope a dim-branded steer, and he went over a thirty-foot cut bank, and they both went over after him. Davis had lost his rope; he was reaching down to pick it up, at a gallop, and he didn't see what was coming. The second man saw it in time. He pulled his horse's head way up, and he lit more or less right side on top. It shook him up something terrible and he spent a long time in the hospital, but he lived through it. Davis was killed deader than hell.

The roundup boys saw all this happen. When they got down there, a rider taken him up in front of his saddle and carried him to camp in his arms. Our outfit laid off that afternoon to rest the herd and help bury him, and I remember after we got the grave dug one of the fellows said: "Somebody ought to say something. Don't nobody know the Lord's Prayer?" I said: "I do." So they asked me to say it over him, but I only got as far as "Thy will be done," and got to thinking about my brother and had to quit. You know why. I was kind of rattled anyhow.

Coming up in '79, we ran into rustlers in the Nations. These fellows were Mexicans and some good-for-nothing white men and half-breeds who picked on the trail herds after they crossed Red River. They would follow you up for days with a packhorse, waiting their chance and keeping out of sight among the hills. A dark night was what they were looking for, especially if it was raining hard, because the rain would wash out the tracks—they'd figured all that out. They would watch you as you rode around the herd on night guard— always two men, and you rode to meet—and then when the two of you come together, they would slip up to the other side of the herd and wave a blanket. And the whole herd would get up like one animal and light out. These rustlers had very good horses, and they would cut in ahead of you as you tried to get up in front of the herd and would cut off anywhere from fifty to two hundred head of big, strong lead steers.

Our outfit saw them just after they had popped the blanket. The fellows on night herd started shooting, and the rest of us woke up and grabbed for our horses. It's funny how long ago it seems. All I remember is a wild goose chase. The rustlers just left our little night horses, and of course they got away with the cattle. But next morning another fellow and I cut for sign and we found their trail. We followed it until we saw a man's hat sticking up over the top of a hill. And on the other side of the hill we found our steers.

We hit the Western trail that trip, crossing Red River at Doan's store, and we came on up to Loup River in Nebraska and turned the cattle over there. After that I went home to see my mother. I had been away a solid year. No, I hadn't wrote to her. Didn't have nothing to tell her—didn't want any of them to know where I was. I was her pet and all that, but she was always bullyragging me about drinking and spending my money in town, and so on—afraid I was going to turn out bad. I thought I knew more than she did. And I didn't know straight up.

But before I went home, I stopped in North Platte, where they paid us off, and bought some new clothes and got that second picture taken. There is nothing long ago about that. I remember it like it was yesterday. I had a new white Stetson hat that I paid ten dollars for and new pants that cost twelve dollars, and a good shirt and fancy boots. They had colored tops, red and blue, with a half-moon and star on them. Lord, I was proud of these clothes! They were the kind of clothes top hands wore, and I thought I was dressed right for the first time in my life. I believe one reason I went home was just so I could show them off.

But when I got there and my sister saw me, she said: "Take your pants out of your boots and put your coat on. You look like an outlaw."

I told her to go to hell. And I never did like her after that. Those were the first store clothes I had ever bought myself. Before that my mother made my clothes or they were bought for me, just like you'd do for a kid.

My sister was a fool anyhow.

I Woke Up Wicked

BY DOROTHY M. JOHNSON

I USED TO RIDE with the Rough String, but not any more. They were tough out-laws, the Rough String; and the lawmen that chased them—from a safe dis-tance—were hard cases too. In fact, everybody around was plumb dangerous except me.

I was just a poor innocent cowboy, broke but not otherwise wicked. I didn't want to join them outlaws, but I was running away from justice—the crookedest justice a man ever did see.

I was twenty-two years old when I rode into Durkee, a cow town in Mon-tana, after helping eight other fellows deliver a trail herd of steers.

"Meet me at the bank in an hour, boys," says the wagon boss. "I'll pay you off there."

We scattered and started strutting the streets, all ragged and dusty. We was too broke to do anything but strut. Anyhow, while I was strutting, I see this fel-low behind a lawman's badge; he's leaning against a wall and looking at me with his eyes narrow. It made me kind of mad, and my heart was pure, so I says, "See anything green? Well, by gosh, if it ain't Cousin Cuthbert! Cuthbert, you shouldn't of ever run off. Your ma's been real upset. . . ."

This fellow's eyes got so narrow I doubt if he could see out of 'em. "I am Buck Sanderson, deputy sheriff of this county, stranger," he said. And then, looking around, he whispers, "How are you, Willie?"

"My name is Duke Jackson," I says, huffy. "Seems like I made a mistake."

"You are a likely looking young fellow," he says, "and you remind me of somebody." He grinned, and I knew that he had got the idea—when I mentioned a mistake—that I meant I was on the run. But I wasn't, not then.

"You got any plans?" he says.

"The crew is gonna get paid off at the bank pretty quick," I says. "After that, I don't know what I'm going to do."

"Well, come have a drink," Cuthbert says. I should have known better than to drink with Cuthbert; he'd been a mean one as far back as anyone could remember. But I had a beer and he had red-eye, and then he says, "I'll mosey along with you to the bank."

"I can find it," I says, but he come anyway.

On the way he stopped by a hitch rack and squinted at a sorrel gelding with a fancy saddle on it. "Now what's the sheriff's horse doing there?" Cuthbert says. "It was supposed to be took to the livery stable, but I guess the hostler forgot. Here, you lead him. I got to keep my gun hand free. This is a tough town."

So I led the sheriff's horse, rather than argue with him. There was some fellas standing in front of the bank, but none of them was from our crew, and there was some horses standing around.

"I'll go see if they're paying off yet," Cuthbert says. "You hold the horse."

"You hold him," I says. "It's me that's getting paid off."

"Hold the horse," he says, and walked into the bank.

So I was standing there, getting mad, when three or four shots blasted out. And then men came boiling out of the bank like hornets and leaped onto those horses that were waiting. Cuthbert came running out with them and after he'd let the men get a start, he began shooting after them but up in the air. Well, I saw that Cuthbert hadn't changed any, and so I did the obvious thing. I jumped on the sheriff's horse and galloped him out of town.

Ten miles out, I stopped to see if any bullets had hit me. They hadn't.

There I was, a refugee from justice. I'd stolen the sheriff's horse, and the bank had been robbed with me standing there looking like I was part of the gang; and I was a witness to the fact that Cuthbert was in on the holdup.

I sat down in some bushes and wished for a smoke and thought what a perfidious villain Cuthbert was. I decided to go back and tell the sheriff so, but not just then. Some other year would do. If I went riding back to Durkee that day, on the sheriff's horse, people might misunderstand.

So I rode another ten miles farther away. It was getting dark then, so I unsaddled and went to bed in the brush, wishing I could eat grass like the sorrel.

I woke up in the dark, only it wasn't as dark as it should have been. Somebody had a fire going, and I could hear voices. Couldn't even get a good night's sleep. I sat up, and somebody says, "That you, Larry?"

"Never heard of him," I says, "and can't you guys shut up?" That just goes to show what a pure heart I had, and how little brains. All of a sudden I recalled that I was a wanted man.

"Got a rifle on you, mister," a man says. "Come into the light with your hands up."

Well, I didn't even stop to pull my boots on.

"How long you been there?" says a man with a black mustache. There was four of them, all with guns.

"How long don't matter," says a man with a beard. "Either he's on our side or he's dead."

"I'm on your side," I says. "Which side is it?"

The man with the beard scowled. "You ever drive cattle on shares?"

"Just for wages," I says. "I'm a hardworking cowpuncher looking for opportunity."

"It has found you," he says. "What name do you go by?"

"Duke," I says.

"No you don't," he says. "I'm Duke." He glared at me in the firelight and says, "You're Leather."

"Why, no such thing," I says. "I'm just ordinary skin like anybody else." Then it dawned on me who Duke was. Everybody knew the name Duke—he was one of the headmen of the Rough String. Fact was, I took the name Duke not long before just because a reputation went with it. "If you say so," I says politely, "I'm Leather."

"Go bring Leather his boots," says Duke. "Give Leather a cup of coffee."

So that was how my name changed to Leather. And that was how I turned outlaw. No trouble at all. Went to bed honest and broke, woke up wicked and still broke, and misunderstood by everybody.

"We'll use you in our cattle business," Duke says. I didn't have to make any decisions at all. Seemed like I was cut out to be an outlaw.

You might think driving stolen cattle was exciting, but it wasn't. They didn't look any different, viewed from the dust of the drags, than they had when I pushed 'em along as a law-abiding citizen. Why should they look any different? They were some of the very same cattle.

After they became rustled cattle, they were easier to move. When they were an honest herd, the trail crew was always running into officious lawmen and nesters that said "You can't bring that herd through here" or "You can't cross this line." But when the Rough String moved them steers, the lawmen were somewheres else on urgent business, and the nesters waited for the Rough String with open arms.

This is the life, I began to think. It's safer and quieter than being an honest cowboy. Nobody gets close enough to point a gun at you.

I could even have enjoyed it if all them outlaws hadn't made me so nervous. Duke and the boys looked like cowboys anywhere, dusty and needing a shave, and red-eyed because with a trail herd you never get enough sleep. But just knowing they were the Rough String made me shiver. I tried being real polite and they glared at me. So I glared back and showed my teeth, and after that we got along pretty good. Being an outlaw is awful tiring on your facial muscles.

We moved them cattle right along because the former owner had men on our trail. When the men got too close, they slowed up and waited for a prudent length of time. Their boss was even safer—he was home on the ranch.

One day we pushed them cattle up to the top of a ridge of rimrock, and Duke says with a happy sigh, "Well, there it is. Eagle Nest."

The boys sat their horses, and we looked down into the prettiest green valley I ever saw. The steers went snorting down the trail to water and that good green grass, and most of the boys went "Yippee!" and spurred their horses down that way too.

"Got girls waiting down there," says Duke, explaining to me. "Now there is a settlement no lawman ever laid eyes on, boy. Eagle Nest. Not that they don't know where it is." He chuckled fondly. "We got a nice layout there. Families, kids. Even had a school till the teacher got married."

Then he yelled, "Yippee!" and off he went.

"I am Leather Jackson," I says out loud to myself. "One of the Rough String. I am a real bad fellow." But I wished my teeth wouldn't chatter.

I yelled, "Yippee!" and spurred my horse down the trail to Eagle Nest. Down there they would protect me. I flung out of the saddle in front of a log building with a hitch rack. I started to swagger in. A dark-skinned girl with long earrings came out, grinned at me.

"You are Leath-air Jackson," she says to me.

I swept off my hat and says, "Yes, ma'am, I sure am, and what might your name be?" Not that I gave a hang, but it occurred to me that the Rough String's womenfolk might be even more dangerous than the outlaws themselves, and one thing you can always do when you meet a strange woman, dangerous or not, is be awful polite.

"My name ees Carmen," she says. She would have been kind of pretty if she hadn't had a front tooth missing.

Just then Duke came, glaring at me and her, so I says, "Pleased to meet you, ma'am," and, "Boss, where do I bunk? Because it's a long, long time since I had a solid night's sleep."

"The big cabin is for the single men," Duke says. "The little shacks is for those of us that's got our own housekeeping arrangements. Carmen, you git along home and don't dally."

She dallied long enough to wave her eyelashes at me, and that raised a chill along the back of my neck.

"Your credit's good at the store here," Duke says, motioning.

That was a relief, because being an outlaw hadn't made me any more prosperous than I was while honest.

The storekeeper squinted at me and says, "I reckon you're Leather Jackson. What'll you have?"

"Soap to get the dust off the outside," I says. "And a can of peaches to cut it on the inside, and some smoking tobacco to relax with before I go to sleep for four or five days." I was a real tough rustler, I was. Still wanted the same old comforts.

While I was drinking the peach juice, my eyes got used to the dim light, and I see there was a woman about ten feet away. I put a little more distance between us, and she says in a ladylike voice, "Mr. Frasier, would you introduce us?"

"Oh, gosh, excuse me," the storekeeper says. "Miz Pickett, meet Leather Jackson, the new man."

I grabbed off my hat and bowed, and she says, "How do you do."

She was a pretty lady, real young, had all her teeth too, but she looked prim and wore a black dress. Now if there was anything you didn't expect to see in Eagle Nest, it was a prim lady.

"I hope we shall become better acquainted," she says, and went out.

"Yes, sir," I says, baffled. "Yes, ma'am, I do too."

Mr. Frasier leaned on the counter and says, "The widow there, she came in here to teach school and married Ed Pickett. He got shot a while back. The other women say she's a snob because she keeps her marriage certificate up on the wall. They're just jealous."

"A very nice lady," I says.

"You bet she is," says Mr. Frasier. "And if you ever find out whether she really did ride with the String when they took the express car at Middle Fork, I sure wish you'd tell me."

I didn't say anything. My teeth were chattering on the rim of the peach can.

Then I could see it all—the poor orphan girl with no folks, lured into that nest of thieves to teach school, falling in love with this bandit, Pickett, then widowed when he was shot. Poor girl.

I put down the empty peach can and throwed my shoulders back and says, "If you want trouble with Leather Jackson, mister, just let me hear you say one evil word about that little lady."

He cringed. "I wouldn't, Leather, I sure wouldn't! I bet it's all a vicious rumor, about her riding with the—"

"That's the kind of evil word I mean," I grated at him, getting my gun out after only one fumble.

He backed off with his hands hovering level with his shoulders. "Just a vicious rumor," he repeated, "and to show you my heart's in the right place, I won't even charge you for that merchandise you just bought."

"I'll let the slander pass this time," I says through my teeth.

I found the bunkhouse, swaggered in like I owned it, growled at the boys, and laid down in a bunk. I slept thirty-six hours and would have stretched it longer except I got hungry.

I woke up mad—and scared—and laid there with my eyes shut, figuring. William Jackson, I says to myself. Duke Jackson. Leather Jackson—now I know you, boy. What you going to do about the jam you're in? You're not the best shot in the world, and your hide's not made of cast iron.

Then I figured out why I was mad, and I was ashamed of being so selfish when there was that unprotected little widow marooned among that bunch of outlaws.

She dassent leave, I figured, because probably the hard-hearted lawmen would get her on account of her associations. She wouldn't have no money to live on if she could escape. And them saying she held up a train!

Well, I worked up such a mad that I wasn't scared no more. I marched out of there in a towering rage, clean forgetting to put on my gun belt, which was in my war sack. Outside I met two or three of the Rough String and glared 'em down. They glanced at my hip—no holster there—and my murderous expression, and they seen a cold-blooded killer who didn't need firearms. Why, Leather Jackson was the type that would throttle an innocent grizzly bear with his raw hands.

They stepped aside for me, they did, and made me welcome.

I never did so much loafing since I got out of my cradle. There was nothing to do but lounge around and gossip and play cards and get drunk. But I didn't wish to drink in that company and was scared to win at cards and was not willing to lose, even if I'd had any money. So I listened, and that got monotonous too. My face got tired from keeping that tough look on it, just waiting for somebody to drop an evil word about poor little Miz Pickett.

They gabbed about old holdups till hell wouldn't have it. Miz Pickett's late husband was horse-holder when they robbed a bank, I learned, and some kid shot him from an upstairs window when they came out with the money.

About once an hour somebody would say with a long face, "I never did believe that nonsense about the widow riding with the boys when they took that train, though," and the rest of them, carefully not looking my way, would chime in, "No, no!" like the Ladies Aid fighting off the idea that the preacher had been seen staggering out of a saloon.

After three or four days, one of Duke's boys gave me the word I was on guard duty that night.

"Take your rifle up to the rim," he says, "and keep it ready. Nobody's tried to bust into Eagle Nest yet, but some lawman out to make a reputation might try it.

"One shot from up there, and we'll all be with you. But don't go shooting just to hear the echo. There's few things make the boys madder than to get routed out of a quiet night's sleep because some green guard gets jumpy and shoots the blazes out of a friendly juniper.

"In fact," he says, "one fellow that done it ain't been seen since."

There was even a password. It was Twenty Dollars.

Night-herding rimrock and juniper trees is even duller than riding around bedded-down cattle. I hummed and whistled and sang and practiced cussing. Then I dozed, setting on a rock with the rifle on my knees.

I woke up with an awful start, hearing horses coming up the trail from the outside. I rolled down behind the rock and yelped, "Who's there?"

A deep voice says, "Who the hell do you think it is? And who are you?"

See, no password. So if he didn't want to give it, I was willing. Nobody told me who was supposed to deal.

"For twenty dollars I'd bore a hole clean through you," I says, big and rough, but protected by that rock. Anyhow I hoped I was.

He says, "Oh, hell, I forgot that. We got lots more than twenty dollars on a led horse here."

So we got acquainted. There was five of them, and they had eighteen thousand dollars in gold coin on a pack horse. We shook hands and had a smoke and then they went on down to Eagle Nest.

I set there shaking like a leaf, because I found out, hiding behind that rock, that I wasn't going to shoot nobody no matter how big I talked about it. Even if they'd all been Cuthbert, I wouldn't have fired. I'd shot lots of game and butchered yearlings that wasn't mine, like any cowboy when the grub's short. I'd even shot a horse once. But I never had shot any people. And damned if I was going to start then, just to protect that bunch of bandits down in Eagle Nest.

It was quite a surprise to find that out, let me tell you. Made me stop and think.

Well, I wasn't hobbled on that rimrock. What's to stop me, I says to myself, from getting on my horse and going down over the side to where the rest of the world is?

Several things stopped me. The Rough String wouldn't like it, though I hadn't taken no blood oath or anything. The law might not like it too well because I still had the sheriff's horse. And if I left, who was going to look out for Miz Pickett? No, I wasn't hobbled. But I was sure ground-tied.

So there I was, a stout young fellow with no bad habits, stuck with them outlaws and helpless to protect the lady. Rustling cattle was no habit with me. I never did drink much, I'd quit gambling, and I was scared of the girls in Eagle Nest—they carried little knives in their garters. All in all, I was a nicer fellow since turning badman. I was way too good for Eagle Nest, but I was scared to pull out.

When I rode down at sunup, Miz Pickett was lugging a couple of buckets of water to her cabin, so I stopped to help. Delicate-looking little thing, she was.

"I'd ask you in to breakfast," she says, "but you know how people talk."

"Ma'am, I would gladly go hungry to protect your good name," I says gallantly, setting down the buckets on her doorsill.

She gave me an approving look, and I noticed something funny. She was such a prim little lady, and she looked at me like my aunt used to, over her glasses. But Miz Pickett didn't have any glasses on.

"Leather," says she, "have you ever thought of quitting this life of banditry?"

Of course, I hadn't thought of much else since I got into it, but I was cautious. Anyhow, if she wanted to reform me, I wanted to give her the satisfaction of having a job to do. "A fellow thinks about a lot of things," I says.

"Crime brings nobody any good. There was my husband, shot down in a bank robbery. Are you any better off since you joined the Rough String?"

"Well, yes," I says. "I've got credit at Mr. Frasier's store."

"But no cash. Not until those steers you brought in are fattened up and sold. And what if the nesters who usually buy them get cold feet? The price on stolen beef goes pretty low."

"Was you thinking of getting out of here, ma'am?" I asked in a whisper. "Not that I want to inquire into your private business."

She looked droopy and pitiful. "I could go back to teaching. But would the Rough String dare to let me leave?"

"Any time you want help, ma'am," I says, big and bold. "Any time you want to go. . . ."

She smiled, sad and sweet. "Thank you, Leather. Thank you for carrying the water."

Less than a week later, Duke said it was my turn on guard again. For a minute—or less, probably—I thought of asking him what those other lazy loafers were going to do with their time and why should I get night duty so soon, but it seemed smarter to show my teeth and answer, "Fine. Maybe a posse will try coming tonight."

So I went up there again on the rimrock, but this time it was some different. Miz Pickett had fixed up a nice lunch for me. I ate away at it in the dark, mourning my misspent past and cloudy future, and yawning and fretting. Then I sat up with a jerk.

There was the sound of a horse down below, on the Eagle Nest side of the rim. No horse in his right mind would be up there in the rocks and brush of his own choice. The Rough String prided itself on good horses; there wasn't a half-wit in the lot. So that horse wasn't there by accident.

Maybe Duke or somebody was testing me out, I thought. I hollered, "Who's there? Come up and lemme look at you or I shoot!" My, I sounded mean. Even scared myself.

A woman's voice says, "Oh, please don't!"

If there was anything I didn't want up there, it was a visit from one of those Eagle Nest girls. I grabbed the sheriff's horse's reins, ready to ride down to the outside into the arms of the law, if I could find any.

Then the voice said, "Leather, please help me. Can you change twenty dollars?" and I went plunging through the brush toward it, because it was Miz Pickett. For her I wouldn't even have needed the password.

She had a saddle horse and a packhorse, and one of them had a hoof caught between two logs. She had come up through the brush instead of on the trail. I yanked him out. I felt so big and strong I could have picked him up and lifted him out if necessary.

"This is the night I'm leaving," Miz Pickett says. "The String is having a big meeting down in the saloon, planning something."

"Let's ride," I says, with my chest puffed up like a balloon. And that was how I left Eagle Nest. Easy enough, once somebody gave me a push.

We could have gone faster if she hadn't brought so much stuff on that packhorse. I didn't even have my war sack, what cowboys used to call their forty years' gatherings, but Miz Pickett had everything—grub and blankets and a couple of wooden boxes roped on. A neater job of packing stuff on a horse I never saw.

"Those are my books in there," she explained when I glanced at the boxes at our first camp stop.

But when I stepped toward the packhorse to start unloading, she says, "Never mind. Get the fire going."

"Sure, I'll get the fire going," I says, "but I wouldn't want you to lift that heavy stuff off the packsaddle."

"Leather," she says, and I turned around. She still looked prim, in a black dress with a divided skirt for riding, but do you know what? She had a gun in her hand, pointed right at me.

"There's some good firewood over there to the left," I says, marching that way in a hurry. Right then I got a strong suspicion there was a mighty few books in them boxes.

Officially, we took turns sleeping, with one awake staying on guard, not necessarily against wandering lawmen. The Eagle Nest boys were going to miss that gold any minute. But Miz Pickett didn't seem to sleep at all. We camped four nights, and every time I moved a muscle while I was on guard, I could feel that she was watching me from where she was supposed to be asleep.

One morning she says, "Another forty miles to the railroad."

"Fine," I says, wondering if she'd dry-gulch me before we got there.

"Ever been in the cattle business on your own?" she asks during coffee by the breakfast fire.

"Never have," I says.

"I think I'll give up schoolteaching," she says, "and raise beef instead. I'll need a foreman."

That girl didn't need a foreman. Everything she needed she already had. But I was in no position to refuse.

"Expect you will, ma'am," I says, and she nodded as if it was all settled.

"I'm going to take the train," she says. "You can come along a week later. I'm your sister, Mary Smith."

"Pleased to meet you sis," I says. "And where should I meet you later?" Not that I was going to, but it seemed wise to act interested.

She wrote down the address, and I put the paper in my shirt pocket.

She smiled her prim little smile and says, "We're going to get along all right in the cattle business, Leather."

I think I'll give up schoolteaching.

I hoped we were, with a thousand miles between us as soon as I could arrange it.

"You'd better hide out," she suggested. "The Rough String must be getting pretty close by now."

"Reckon so," I agreed. She didn't recommend any place for me to hide. With the law ahead, and the String hot on the trail behind, what was a poor cowboy to do that was wanted for bank robbery, cattle rustling, and stealing the sheriff's sorrel horse?

"By the way," I says, "where do you figure to catch your train?"

"Durkee," she says.

I jumped a foot. "Durkee! Hell—excuse me, ma'am—shucks, I can't go to Durkee! That's where the bank was held up while I was holding this horse right in front of it, and this horse belongs to the sheriff."

She looked annoyed. I sure hated to annoy Miz Pickett.

"Durkee is where I intend to get the train," she says. "My goodness, do you think you're so outstanding that anybody's going to recognize you?"

She had a sound argument there. I did look like an ordinary feller now I'd stopped scowling at the Rough String and let my face hang loose. And if Cuthbert was around, was he going to identify me? He certainly was not. I'd identify him right back.

"There's a man in Durkee I'd like to meet sometime," she says thoughtfully. "I don't know for sure who he is, but he's a cunning wretch. He engineered a bank holdup there that the Rough String got the blame for. The String didn't hold up that bank."

"No, ma'am, they didn't," I says. "They were rustling cattle."

We made it to the depot just ahead of the train. As I was snatching at the ropes on the packsaddle, I glanced at the loafers by the depot, and cold chills went up my spine, because there was Cuthbert behind his nickel-plated star. But I preferred his company to Miz Pickett's. Also to the Rough String, and they might catch up with me any time, now she was going to leave me with no protection but my own wits.

"Good-bye, Harry, take care of yourself," says Little Rattlesnake, and I hoisted her boxes on the train.

"My books," I heard her tell the conductor.

The train started chugging, and I heard my second cousin say behind me, "Hello, Duke."

Cuthbert has got a nice safe jail, I says to myself. That's one place the Rough String won't come looking for me. I says, "Hello, Buck."

"Who's the girl?" he says.

"My sister," I says.

"I know your sisters, Willie, and she ain't one of 'em," he says. "You always were a liar."

So I hit him, but not very hard. He grappled me, and I fought just a bit.

"Resisting an officer, eh?" he says, yanking his gun out and relieving me of mine. "March right along, Willie, and if you tell anyone we're related, I'll shoot you."

"I'd rather be shot than admit it," I says, marching so fast he had to trot to keep up with me.

I was sure glad to get in that jail.

"Now we'll see what you got in your pockets," says Cuthbert. "H'm, broke, of course. What's this piece of paper here in your shirt pocket? I bet that's the address of the girl you put on the train."

"Don't take that!" I says. "I'll never remember where I'm to meet her."

He backed off, grinning, with the paper in his hand. "And why should she want you to meet her?" he says.

"Don't know as she does," I says, "but she's my golden future. She's not only pretty, she's also rich and wants a foreman for her ranch."

"Shouldn't be hard to find her a good man," says Cuthbert, tilting his hat.

"She said she'd sure like to meet you," I says, "but if you was to go climb on that train, it would be just plain dirty of you, because I seen her first." The train tooted and Cuthbert grinned.

"Stay here, Willie boy," he says.

He plumb forgot to lock the door, but I stayed in the cell. I stayed and stayed and stayed.

Around suppertime an older man came in. "What you doing here?"

"Was put here by a fellow with a star on," I says.

"Ain't nothing wrote down in the book," he says. "What you in for?"

"Hitting him, I guess," I says.

"Often wanted to do it myself," says the man. "You can go, for all I care."

Was there no refuge for Willie Jackson, the reformed outlaw?

"I'm wanted in nine states and some territories," I says. "Robbing banks, rustling cattle, forgery, arson—and stealing horses! Why, I've got a horse that belongs to the sheriff right now!"

"You have!" he says, grinning. "Why, boy, I'm so glad to find that horse, you know what I'm going to do? I'm going to make you a deputy. Somebody said they seen Buck get on the train, so I'm going to need a new deputy. We got some big game coming in here. You know who's coming? Eight members of the Rough String, that's who. Got fourteen more of 'em divided up among two other counties, and we get the overflow. Telegram just came in about how they run into a posse that was looking for somebody else. You want to work for me?"

"My health ain't good," I says. "I get the leaping flitters."

He yelled down the street after me, "Hey, you forgot your gun and your hat," so I had to delay long enough to go back and get them.

"Yes, sir," the sheriff says, "they got just about all the Rough String except the little lady that was boss of the whole shebang. Five thousand dollars' reward for her, but nobody outside the outlaws knows what she looks like."

"Five feet two," I says, "dark hair, looks like the president of the Ladies Aid. She took the same train out as your deputy. That's why he was on it."

"Whoof!" says the sheriff and left without warning. I was right behind him, but I passed him when he swung into the telegraph office. His horse was ten yards farther on.

It was a year or so, I guess, before they stopped looking for me, the unidentified cowboy riding the sheriff's horse who set the law on Miz Pickett and perfidious Cuthbert. If I'd turned myself in to be a witness, I could have been a hero. But I always felt kind of guilty about Cuthbert, and anyhow, you never knew which ones of the Rough String would break out of the penitentiary next.

Miz Pickett broke out and got away to South America. I was sure relieved to read about it in a newspaper, though I never had nothing against the South Americans. But they saved me from having to run off to some heathen place like China to stay clear of Miz Pickett. I went home to Pennsylvania and took up plowing.

The Bandana

By J. Frank Dobie

Modern cowboys seem to be giving up the bandana handkerchief. Perhaps the moving pictures have made it tawdry. Yet there was a time when this article was almost as necessary to a cowboy's equipment as a rope, and it served for purposes almost as varied. The prevailing color of the bandana was red, but blues and blacks were common, and of course silk bandanas were prized above those made of cotton.

When the cowboy got up in the morning and went down to the water hole to wash his face, he used his bandana for a towel. Then he tied it around his neck, letting the fold hang down in front, thus appearing rather nattily dressed for breakfast. After he had roped out his bronc and tried to bridle him, he probably found that the horse had to be blindfolded before he could do anything with him. The bandana was what he used to blindfold the horse with. Mounted, the cowboy removed the blind from the horse and put it again around his own neck. Perhaps he rode only a short distance before he spied a big calf that should be branded. He roped the calf; then if he did not have a "piggin string"—a short rope used for tying down animals—he tied the calf's legs together with the bandana and thus kept the calf fast while he branded it. In the summertime, the cowboy adjusted the bandana to protect his neck from the sun. He often wore gloves too, for he liked to present neat hands and neck. If the hot sun was in his face, he adjusted the bandana in front of him, tying it so that the fold would hang over his cheeks, nose, and mouth like a mask. If his business was with a dust-raising herd of cattle, the bandana adjusted in the

The flag of the range country.

same way made a respirator; in blizzardy weather it likewise protected his face and ears. In the swift, unhalting work required in the pen, the cowboy could, without losing time, grab a fold of the bandana loosely hung about his neck and wipe away the blinding sweat. In the pen, too, the bandana served as a rag for holding the hot handles of branding irons.

Many a cowboy has spread his bandana, perhaps none too clean itself, over dirty, muddy water and used it as a strainer to drink through; sometimes he used it as a cup towel, which he called a "drying rag." If the bandana was dirty, it was probably not so dirty as the other apparel of the cowboy, for when he came to a hole of water, he was wont to dismount and wash out his handkerchief, letting it dry while he rode along, holding it in his hand or spread over his hat. Often he wore it under his hat in order to help keep his head cool. At other times, in the face of a fierce gale, he used it to tie down his hat. The bandana made a good sling for a broken arm; it made a good bandage for a blood wound. Early Irish settlers on the Nueces River used to believe that a bandana handkerchief that had been worn by a drowned man would, if cast into a stream above the sunken body, float until it came over the body and then sink, thus locating it. Many a cowboy out on the lonely plains has been buried with a clean bandana spread over his face to keep the dirt, or the coarse blanket on which the dirt was poured, from touching it. The bandana has been used to hang men with. Rustlers used to "wave" strangers around with it, as a warning against nearer approach, though the hat was more commonly used for signaling. Like the Mexican sombrero or the four-gallon Stetson, the bandana could not be made too large. When the cowboys of the West make their final parade on the grassy shores of Paradise, the guidon that leads them should be a bandana handkerchief. It deserves to be called the flag of the range country.

From *The Virginian*

By Owen Wister

"Glad to see yu've got your gun with you," continued the happy fool. "You know what Trampas claims about that affair of yours in the Tetons? He claims that if everything was known about the killing of Shorty—"

"Take one on the house," suggested the proprietor to him, amiably. "Your news will be fresher." And he pushed him the bottle. The fool felt less important.

"This talk had went the rounds before it got to us," said Scipio, "or we'd have headed it off. He has got friends in town."

Perplexity knotted the Virginian's brows. This community knew that a man had implied he was a thief and a murderer; it also knew that he knew it. But the case was one of peculiar circumstances, assuredly. Could he avoid meeting the man? Soon the stage would be starting south for the railroad. He had already today proposed to his sweetheart that they should take it. Could he for her sake leave unanswered a talking enemy upon the field? His own ears had not heard the enemy.

Into these reflections the fool stepped once more. "Of course this country don't believe Trampas," said he. "This country—"

But he contributed no further thoughts. From somewhere in the rear of the building, where it opened upon the tin cans and the hinder purlieus of the town, came a movement, and Trampas was among them, courageous with whiskey.

All the fools now made themselves conspicuous. One lay on the floor, knocked there by the Virginian, whose arm he had attempted to hold. Others struggled with Trampas, and his bullet smashed the ceiling before they could drag the pistol from him. "There now! there now!" they interposed; "you don't want to talk like that," for he was pouring out a tide of hate and vilification. Yet the Virginian stood quiet by the bar, and many an eye of astonishment was turned upon him. "I'd not stand half that language," some muttered to each other. Still the Virginian waited quietly, while the fools reasoned with Trampas. But no earthly foot can step between a man and his destiny. Trampas broke suddenly free.

"Your friends have saved your life," he rang out, with obscene epithets. "I'll give you till sundown to leave town."

There was total silence instantly.

"Trampas," spoke the Virginian, "I don't want trouble with you."

"He never has wanted it," Trampas sneered to the bystanders. "He has been dodging it five years. But I've got him corralled."

Some of the Trampas faction smiled

"Trampas," said the Virginian again, "are yu' sure yu' really mean that?"

The whiskey bottle flew through the air, hurled by Trampas, and crashed through the saloon window behind the Virginian.

"That was surplusage, Trampas," said he, "if yu mean the other."

"Get out by sundown, that's all," said Trampas. And wheeling, he went out of the saloon by the rear, as he had entered.

"Gentlemen," said the Virginian, "I know you will all oblige me."

"Sure!" exclaimed the proprietor, heartily. "We'll see that everybody lets this thing alone."

The Virginian gave a general nod to the company, and walked out into the street.

———

The Virginian unlocked the room in the hotel where he kept stored his tent, his blankets, his packsaddles, and his many accoutrements for the bridal journey in the mountains. Out of the window he saw the mountains blue in shadow, but some cottonwoods distant in the flat between were still bright green in the sun. From among his possessions he took quickly a pistol, wiping and loading it. Then from its holster he removed the pistol which he had tried and made sure of in the morning. This, according to his wont when going into a risk, he shoved between his trousers and his shirt in front. The untried weapon he placed in the holster, letting it hang visibly at his hip. He glanced out of the window again and saw the mountains of the same deep blue. But the cottonwoods were no longer in the sunlight. The shadow had come past them, nearer the town; for fifteen of the forty minutes were gone. "The bishop is wrong," he said. "There is no sense in telling her." And he turned to the door, just as she came to it herself.

"Oh!" she cried out at once, and rushed to him.

He swore as he held her close. "The fools!" he said. "The fools!"

"It has been so frightful waiting for you," said she, leaning her head against him.

"Who had to tell you this?" he demanded.

"I don't know. Somebody just came and said it."

"This is mean luck," he murmured, patting her. "This is mean luck."

She went on: "I wanted to run out and find you; but I didn't! I didn't! I stayed quiet in my room till they said you had come back."

"It is mean luck. Mighty mean," he repeated.

"How could you be so long?" she asked. "Never mind, I've got you now. It is over."

Anger and sorrow filled him. "I might have known some fool would tell you," he said.

"It's all over. Never mind." Her arms tightened their hold of him. Then she let him go. "What shall we do?" she said. "What now?"

"Now?" he answered. "Nothing now."

She looked at him without understanding.

"I know it is a heap worse for you," he pursued, speaking slowly. "I knew it would be."

"But it is over!" she exclaimed again.

He did not understand her now. He kissed her. "Did you think it was over?" he said simply. "There is some waiting still before us. I wish you did not have to wait alone. But it will not be long." He was looking down, and did not see the happiness grow chilled upon her face and then fade into bewildered fear. "I did my best," he went on. "I think I did. I know I tried. I let him say to me before them all what no man has ever said, or ever will again. I kept thinking hard of you—with all my might, or I reckon I'd have killed him right there.

And I gave him a show to change his mind. I gave it to him twice. I spoke as quiet as I am speaking to you now. But he stood to it. And I expect he knows he went too far in the hearing of others to go back on his threat. He will have to go on to the finish now."

"The finish?" she echoed, almost voiceless.

"Yes," he answered very gently.

Her dilated eyes were fixed upon him. "But—" she could scarce form utterance, "but you?"

"I have got myself ready," he said. "Did you think—why, what did you think?"

She recoiled a step. "What are you going—" She put her two hands to her head. "Oh, God!" she almost shrieked, "you are going—" He made a step, and would have put his arm round her, but she backed against the wall, staring speechless at him.

"I am not going to let him shoot me," he said quietly.

"You mean—you mean—but you can come away!" she cried. "It's not too late yet. You can take yourself out of his reach. Everybody knows that you are brave. What is he to you? You can leave him in this place. I'll go with you anywhere. To any house, to the mountains, to anywhere away. We'll leave this horrible place together and—and—oh, won't you listen to me?" She stretched her hands to him. "Won't you listen?"

He took her hands. "I must stay here."

Her hands clung to his. "No, no, no. There's something else. There's something better than shedding blood in cold blood. Only think what it means! Only think of having to remember such a thing! Why, it's what they hang people for! It's murder!"

He dropped her hands. "Don't call it that name," he said sternly.

"When there was the choice!" she exclaimed, half to herself, like a person stunned and speaking to the air. "To get ready for it when you have the choice!"

"He did the choosing," answered the Virginian. "Listen to me. Are you listening?" he asked, for her gaze was dull.

She nodded.

"I work hyeh. I belong hyeh. It's my life. If folks came to think I was a coward—"

"Who would think you were a coward?"

"Everybody. My friends would be sorry and ashamed, and my enemies would walk around saying they had always said so. I could not hold up my head again among enemies or friends."

"When it was explained—"

"There'd be nothing to explain. There'd just be the fact." He was nearly angry.

"There is a higher courage than fear of outside opinion," said the New England girl.

Her Southern lover looked at her. "Cert'nly there is. That's what I'm showing in going against yours."

"But if you know that you are brave, and if I know that you are brave, oh, my dear, my dear! what difference does the world make? How much higher courage to go your own course—"

"I am goin' my own course," he broke in. "Can't yu' see how it must be about a man? It's not for their benefit, friends or enemies, that I have got this thing to do. If any man happened to say I was a thief and I heard about it, would I let him go on spreadin' such a thing of me? Don't I owe my own honesty something better than that? Would I sit down in a corner rubbin' my honesty and whisperin' to it, 'There! there! I know you ain't a thief'? No, seh; not a little bit! What men say about my nature is not just merely an outside thing. For the fact that I let 'em keep on sayin' it is a proof I don't value my nature enough to shield it from their slander and give them their punishment. And that's being a poor sort of a jay."

She had grown very white.

"Can't yu' see how it must be about a man?" he repeated.

"I cannot," she answered, in a voice that scarcely seemed her own. "If I ought to, I cannot. To shed blood in cold blood. When I heard about that last fall,—about the killing of those cattle thieves,—I kept saying to myself: 'He had to do it. It was a public duty.' And lying sleepless I got used to Wyoming being different from Vermont. But this—"she gave a shudder—"when I think of tomorrow, of you and me, and of—If you do this, there can be no tomorrow for you and me."

At these words he also turned white.

"Do you mean—" he asked, and could go no farther.

Nor could she answer him, but turned her head away.

"This would be the end?" he asked.

Her head faintly moved to signify yes.

He stood still, his hand shaking a little. "Will you look at me and say that?" he murmured at length. She did not move. "Can you do it?" he said.

His sweetness made her turn, but could not pierce her frozen resolve. She gazed at him across the great distance of her despair.

"Then it is really so?" he said.

Her lips tried to form words, but failed.

He looked out of the window and saw nothing but shadow. The blue of the mountains was now become a deep purple. Suddenly his hand closed hard.

"Good-bye, then," he said.

At that word she was at his feet, clutching him. "For my sake," she begged him. "For my sake."

A tremble passed through his frame. She felt his legs shake as she held them, and, looking up, she saw that his eyes were closed with misery. Then he opened them, and in their steady look she read her answer. He unclasped her hands from holding him and raised her to her feet.

"I have no right to kiss you any more," he said. And then, before his desire could break him down from this, he was gone, and she was alone.

She did not fall, or totter, but stood motionless. And next—it seemed a moment and it seemed eternity—she heard in the distance a shot, and then two shots. Out of the window she saw people beginning to run. At that she turned and fled to her room and flung herself face downward upon the floor.

———

The Virginian, for precaution, did not walk out of the front door of the hotel. He went through back ways, and paused once. Against his breast he felt the wedding ring where he had it suspended by a chain from his neck. His hand went up to it, and he drew it out and looked at it. He took it off the chain, and his arm went back to hurl it from him as far as he could. But he stopped and kissed it with one sob and thrust it in his pocket. Then he walked out into the open, watching. He saw men here and there, and they let him pass as before, without speaking. He saw his three friends, and they said no word to him. But they turned and followed in his rear at a little distance, because it was known that Shorty had been found shot from behind. The Virginian gained a position soon where no one could come at him except from in front; and the sight of the mountains was almost more than he could endure, because it was there that he had been going tomorrow.

"It is quite awhile after sunset," he heard himself say.

A wind seemed to blow his sleeve off his arm, and he replied to it and saw Trampas pitch forward. He saw Trampas raise his arm from the ground and fall again, and lie there this time, still. A little smoke was rising from the pistol on the ground, and he looked at his own, and saw the smoke flowing upward out of it.

"I expect that's all," he said aloud.

But as he came nearer Trampas, he covered him with his weapon. He stopped a moment, seeing the hand on the ground move. Two fingers twitched and then ceased; for it was all. The Virginian stood looking down at Trampas.

"Both of mine hit," he said, once more aloud. "His must have gone mighty close to my arm. I told her it would not be me."

He had scarcely noticed that he was being surrounded and congratulated. His hand was being shaken, and he saw it was Scipio in tears. Scipio's joy made his heart like lead within him. He was near telling his friend everything, but he did not.

"If anybody wants me about this," he said, "I will be at the hotel."

"Who'll want you?" said Scipio. "Three of us saw his gun out." And he vented his admiration. "You were that cool! That quick!"

"I'll see you boys again," said the Virginian, heavily, and he walked away.

Scipio looked after him, astonished. "Yu' might suppose he was in poor luck," he said to McLean.

The Virginian walked to the hotel and stood on the threshold of his sweetheart's room. She had heard his step and was upon her feet. Her lips were parted, and her eyes fixed on him, nor did she move, or speak.

"Yu' have to know it," said he. "I have killed Trampas."

"Oh, thank God!" she said; and he found her in his arms. Long they embraced without speaking, and what they whispered then with their kisses matters not.

Both of mine hit.

Thus did her New England conscience battle to the end and, in the end, capitulate to love. And the next day, with the bishop's blessing, and Mrs. Taylor's broadest smile, and the ring on her finger, the Virginian departed with his bride into the mountains.

Wine on the Desert

By Max Brand

THERE WAS NO HURRY, except for the thirst, like clotted salt, in the back of his throat, and Durante rode on slowly, rather enjoying the last moments of dryness before he reached the cold water in Tony's house. There was really no hurry at all. He had almost twenty-four hours' head start, for they would not find his dead man until this morning. After that, there would be perhaps several hours of delay before the sheriff gathered a sufficient posse and started on his trail. Or perhaps the sheriff would be fool enough to come alone.

Durante had been able to see the wheel and fan of Tony's windmill for more than an hour, but he could not make out the ten acres of the vineyard until he had topped the last rise, for the vines had been planted in a hollow. The lowness of the ground, Tony used to say, accounted for the water that gathered in the well during the wet season. The rains sank through the desert sand, through the gravels beneath, and gathered in a bowl of clay hardpan far below.

In the middle of the rainless season the well ran dry, but, long before that, Tony had every drop of the water pumped up into a score of tanks made of cheap corrugated iron. Slender pipelines carried the water from the tanks to the vines and, from time to time, let them sip enough life to keep them until the winter darkened overhead suddenly, one November day, and the rain came down, and all the earth made a great hushing sound as it drank. Durante had heard that whisper of drinking when he was here before; but he never had seen the place in the middle of the long drought.

The windmill looked like a sacred emblem to Durante, and the twenty stodgy, tar-painted tanks blessed his eyes; but a heavy sweat broke out at once from his body. For the air of the hollow, unstirred by wind, was hot and still as a bowl of soup. A reddish soup. The vines were powdered with thin red dust, also. They were wretched, dying things to look at, for the grapes had been gathered, the new wine had been made, and now the leaves hung in ragged tatters.

Durante rode up to the squat adobe house and right through the entrance into the patio. A flowering vine clothed three sides of the little court. Durante did not know the name of the plant, but it had large white blossoms with golden hearts that poured sweetness on the air. Durante hated the sweetness. It made him more thirsty.

He threw the reins off his mule and strode into the house. The watercooler stood in the hall outside the kitchen. There were two jars made of a porous stone, very ancient things, and the liquid which distilled through the pores kept the contents cool. The jar on the left held water; that on the right contained wine. There was a big tin dipper hanging on a peg beside each jar. Durante tossed off the cover of the vase on the left and plunged it in until the delicious coolness closed well above his wrist.

"Hey, Tony," he called. Out of his dusty throat the cry was, "Throw some water into that mule of mine, would you, Tony?"

A voice pealed from the distance.

Durante, pouring down the second dipper of water, smelled the alkali dust that had shaken off his own clothes. It seemed to him that heat was radiating like light from his clothes, from his body, and the cool dimness of the house was soaking it up. He heard the wooden leg of Tony bumping on the ground, and Durante grinned; then Tony came in with that hitch and side-swing with which he accommodated the stiffness of his artificial leg. His brown face shone with sweat as though a special ray of light were focused on it.

"Ah, Dick!" he said. "Good old Dick! . . . How long since you came last! . . . Wouldn't Julia be glad! Wouldn't she be glad!"

"Ain't she here?" asked Durante, jerking his head suddenly away from the dripping dipper.

"She's away at Nogalez," said Tony. "It gets so hot. I said, 'You go up to Nogalez, Julia, where the wind don't forget to blow.' She cried, but I made her go."

"Did she cry?" asked Durante.

"Julia . . . that's a good girl," said Tony.

"Yeah. You bet she's good," said Durante. He put the dipper quickly to his lips but did not swallow for a moment; he was grinning too widely. Afterward he said: "You wouldn't throw some water into that mule of mine, would you, Tony?"

Tony went out with his wooden leg clumping loud on the wooden floor, softly in the patio dust. Durante found the hammock in the corner of the patio. He lay down in it and watched the color of sunset flush the mists of desert dust that rose to the zenith. The water was soaking through his body; hunger began, and then the rattling of pans in the kitchen and the cheerful cry of Tony's voice:

"What you want, Dick? I got some pork. You don't want pork. I'll make you some good Mexican beans. Hot. Ah ha, I know that old Dick. I have plenty of good wine for you, Dick. Tortillas. Even Julia can't make tortillas like me. . . . And what about a nice young rabbit?"

"All blowed full of buckshot?" growled Durante.

"No, no. I kill them with the rifle."

"You kill rabbits with a rifle?" repeated Durante, with a quick interest.

"It's the only gun I have," said Tony. "If I catch them in the sights, they are dead. . . . A wooden leg cannot walk very far. . . . I must kill them quick. You see? They come close to the house about sunrise and flop their ears. I shoot through the head."

"Yeah? Yeah?" muttered Durante. "Through the head?" He relaxed, scowling. He passed his hand over his face, over his head.

Then Tony began to bring the food out into the patio and lay it on a small wooden table; a lantern hanging against the wall of the house included the table in a dim half-circle of light. They sat there and ate. Tony had scrubbed himself for the meal. His hair was soaked in water and sleeked back over his round skull. A man in the desert might be willing to pay five dollars for as much water as went to the soaking of that hair.

Everything was good. Tony knew how to cook, and he knew how to keep the glasses filled with his wine.

"This is old wine. This is my father's wine. Eleven years old," said Tony. "You look at the light through it. You see that brown in the red? That's the soft that time puts in good wine, my father always said."

"What killed your father?" asked Durante.

Tony lifted his hand as though he were listening or as though he were pointing out a thought.

"The desert killed him. I found his mule. It was dead, too. There was a leak in the canteen. My father was only five miles away when the buzzards showed him to me."

"Five miles? Just an hour . . . Good Lord!" said Durante. He stared with big eyes. "Just dropped down and died?" he asked.

"No," said Tony. "When you die of thirst, you always die just one way. . . . First you tear off your shirt, then your undershirt. That's to be cooler. . . . And the sun comes and cooks your bare skin. . . . And then you think . . . there is water everywhere, if you dig down far enough. You begin to dig. The dust comes up your nose. You start screaming. You break your nails in the sand. You wear the flesh off the tips of your fingers, to the bone." He took a quick swallow of wine.

"Without you seen a man die of thirst, how d'you know they start to screaming?" asked Durante.

"They got a screaming look when you find them," said Tony. "Take some more wine. The desert never can get to you here. My father showed me the way to keep the desert away from the hollow. We live pretty good here? No?"

"Yeah," said Durante, loosening his shirt collar. "Yeah, pretty good."

———

Afterward he slept well in the hammock until the report of a rifle waked him and he saw the color of dawn in the sky. It was such a great, round bowl that for a moment he felt as though he were above, looking down into it.

He got up and saw Tony coming in holding a rabbit by the ears, the rifle in his other hand.

"You see?" said Tony. "Breakfast came and called on us!" He laughed.

Durante examined the rabbit with care. It was nice and fat and it had been shot through the head. Through the middle of the head. Such a shudder went down the back of Durante that he washed gingerly before breakfast; he felt that his blood was cooled for the entire day.

It was a good breakfast, too, with flapjacks and stewed rabbit with green peppers, and a quart of strong coffee. Before they had finished, the sun struck through the east window and started them sweating.

"Gimme a look at that rifle of yours, Tony, will you?" Durante asked.

"You take a look at my rifle, but don't you steal the luck that's in it," laughed Tony. He brought the fifteen-shot Winchester.

There was a leak in the canteen.

"Loaded right to the brim?" asked Durante.

"I always load it full the minute I get back home," said Tony.

"Tony, come outside with me," commanded Durante.

They went out from the house. The sun turned the sweat of Durante to hot water and then dried his skin so that his clothes felt transparent.

"Tony, I gotta be damn mean," said Durante. "Stand right there where I can see you. Don't try to get close. . . . Now listen. . . . The sheriff's gunna be along this trail some time today, looking for me. He'll load up himself and all his gang with water out of your tanks. Then he'll follow my sign across the desert. Get me? He'll follow if he finds water on the place. But he's not gunna find water."

"What you done, poor Dick?" said Tony. "Now look. . . . I could hide you in the old wine cellar where nobody . . ."

"The sheriff's not gunna find any water," said Durante. "It's gunna be like this."

He put the rifle to his shoulder, aimed, fired. The shot struck the base of the nearest tank, ranging down through the bottom. A semicircle of darkness began to stain the soil near the edge of the iron wall.

Tony fell on his knees. "No, no, Dick! Good Dick!" he said. "Look! All the vineyard. It will die. It will turn into old, dead wood, Dick. . . ."

"Shut your face," said Durante. "Now I've started, I kinda like the job."

Tony fell on his face and put his hands over his ears. Durante drilled a bullet hole through the tanks, one after another. Afterward, he leaned on the rifle.

"Take my canteen and go in and fill it with water out of the cooling jar," he said. "Snap into it, Tony!"

Tony got up. He raised the canteen and looked around him, not at the tanks from which the water was pouring so that the noise of the earth drinking was audible, but at the rows of his vineyard. Then he went into the house.

Durante mounted his mule. He shifted the rifle to his left hand and drew out the heavy Colt from its holster. Tony came dragging back to him, his head down. Durante watched Tony with a careful revolver but he gave up the canteen without lifting his eyes.

"The trouble with you, Tony," said Durante, "is you're yellow. I'd of fought a tribe of wildcats with my bare hands before I'd let 'em do what I'm doin' to you. But you sit back and take it."

Tony did not seem to hear. He stretched out his hands to the vines.

"Ah, my God," said Tony. "Will you let them all die?"

Durante shrugged his shoulders. He shook the canteen to make sure that it was full. It was so brimming that there was hardly room for the liquid to make a sloshing sound. Then he turned the mule and kicked it into a dogtrot.

Half a mile from the house of Tony, he threw the empty rifle to the ground. There was no sense packing that useless weight, and Tony with his peg leg would hardly come this far.

Durante looked back, a mile or so later, and saw the little image of Tony picking up the rifle from the dust, then staring earnestly after his guest. Durante remembered the neat little hole clipped through the head of the rabbit. Wherever he went, his trail never could return again to the vineyard in the desert. But then, commencing to picture to himself the arrival of the sweating sheriff and his posse at the house of Tony, Durante laughed heartily.

The sheriff's posse could get plenty of wine, of course, but without water a man could not hope to make the desert voyage, even with a mule or a horse to help him on the way. Durante patted the full, rounding side of his canteen. He might even now begin with the first sip, but it was a luxury to postpone pleasure until desire became greater.

He raised his eyes along the trail. Close by, it was merely dotted with occasional bones, but distance joined the dots into an unbroken chalk line, which wavered with a strange leisure across the Apache Desert, pointing toward the cool blue promise of the mountains. The next morning he would be among them.

A coyote whisked out of a gully and ran like a gray puff of dust on the wind. His tongue hung out like a little red rag from the side of his mouth; and suddenly Durante was dry to the marrow. He uncorked and lifted his canteen. It had a slightly sour smell; perhaps the sacking which covered it had grown a trifle old. And then he poured a great mouthful of lukewarm liquid. He had swallowed it before his senses could give him warning.

It was wine!

He looked first of all toward the mountains. They were as calmly blue, as distant as when he had started that morning. Twenty-four hours not on water, but on wine!

"I deserve it," said Durante. "I trusted him to fill the canteen. . . . I deserve it. Curse him!" With a mighty resolution, he quieted the panic in his soul. He would not touch the stuff until noon. Then he would take one discreet sip. He would win through.

Hours went by. He looked at his watch and found it was only ten o'clock. And he had thought that it was on the verge of noon! He uncorked the wine and drank freely and, corking the canteen, felt almost as though he needed a drink of water more than before. He sloshed the contents of the canteen. Already it was horribly light.

Once, he turned the mule and considered the return trip; but he could remember the head of the rabbit too clearly, drilled right through the center. The vineyard, the rows of old twisted, gnarled little trunks with the bark peeling off . . . every vine was to Tony like a human life. And Durante had condemned them all to death!

He faced the blue of the mountains again. His heart raced in his breast with terror. Perhaps it was fear and not the suction of that dry and deadly air that made his tongue cleave to the roof of his mouth.

The day grew old. Nausea began to work in his stomach, nausea alternating with sharp pains. When he looked down, he saw that there was blood on his boots. He had been spurring the mule until the red ran down from its flanks. It went with a curious stagger, like a rocking horse with a broken rocker; and Durante grew aware that he had been keeping the mule at a gallop for a long time. He pulled it to a halt. It stood with wide-braced legs. Its head was down. When he leaned from the saddle, he saw that its mouth was open.

"It's gunna die," said Durante. "It's gunna die. . . . What a fool I been. . . ."

The mule did not die until after sunset. Durante left everything except his revolver. He packed the weight of that for an hour and discarded it in turn. His knees were growing weak. When he looked up at the stars they shone white and clear for a moment only, and then whirled into little racing circles and scrawls of red.

He lay down. He kept his eyes closed and waited for the shaking to go out of his body, but it would not stop. And every breath of darkness was like an inhalation of black dust.

He got up and went on, staggering. Sometimes he found himself running.

Before you die of thirst, you go mad. He kept remembering that. His tongue had swollen big. Before it choked him, if he lanced it with his knife, the blood would help him; he would be able to swallow. Then he remembered that the taste of blood is salty.

Once, in his boyhood, he had ridden through a pass with his father, and they had looked down on the sapphire of a mountain lake, a hundred thousand million tons of water as cold as snow. . . .

When he looked up, now, there were not stars; and this frightened him terribly. He never had seen a desert night so dark. His eyes were failing, he was being blinded. When the morning came, he would not be able to see the mountains, and he would walk around and around in a circle until he dropped and died.

No stars, no wind; the air as still as the waters of a stale pool, and he in the dregs at the bottom. . . .

He seized his shirt at the throat and tore it away so that it hung in two rags from his hips.

He could see the earth only well enough to stumble on the rocks. But there were no stars in the heavens. He was blind: He had no more hope than a rat in a well. Ah, but Italian devils know how to put poison in wine that will steal all the senses or any one of them: And Tony had chosen to blind Durante.

He heard a sound like water. It was the swishing of the soft deep sand through which he was treading; sand so soft that a man could dig it away with his bare hands. . . .

———

Afterward, after many hours, out of the blind face of the sky the rain began to fall. It made first a whispering and then a delicate murmur like voices conversing, but after that, just at the dawn, it roared like the hooves of ten thousand charging horses. Even through that thundering confusion, the big birds with naked heads and red, raw necks found their way down to one place in the Apache Desert.

From *Biting the Dust*

By Dirk Johnson

Unlike any other athlete, the rodeo cowboy must pay to compete. Each contest requires an entry fee, from $25 to more than $300. Travel and lodging costs cut deep into winnings, so cowboys cut corners by riding together and cramming into cheap motel rooms, often two to a bed, or sleeping outdoors.

A share of the prize money comes from ticket sales and fees on advertisers, like Royal Crown whiskey and Copenhagen chewing tobacco. But the bulk of the purse comes out of the cowboys' own pockets, the $12 million in fees paid by some 7,000 rodeo contestants, and 3 percent of that goes to the sport's corporate headquarters, the Pro Rodeo Cowboy Association in Colorado Springs.

The cowboys also pay annual dues of $260 and an insurance fee of $190 per year and $3 per rodeo. The benefits cover only injuries suffered inside the arena, or on the road between contests, and are limited to $12,500. The deductible is $500, and coverage does not extend to family members.

An ambulance always sits parked near the chute gates. Cowboys do not wonder if they will become badly hurt, but when. Rodeo promoters boast that, on average, only one cowboy a year gets killed, although some years are worse than others. The promoters do not keep figures on cowboys who become paralyzed in a crash or retire with a bad limp before age thirty.

And for all the risks, most cowboys scarcely make enough to survive. A rodeo cowboy can become a star and never earn more than $50,000 a year before expenses. Some of the sport's biggest celebrities live in house trailers.

Only one contestant in rodeo makes big money, the All-Around Cowboy, the man who wins the most points in three events or more, the rodeo equivalent of the Olympic decathlon. But even the champ's $250,000 winnings fall well short of the salary of the average benchwarmer in the NBA.

Like his predecessor on the range, the typical rodeo cowboy comes from a working-class background. Often a family ranch or farm looms somewhere in his past. It might have been sold or lost in a bank auction. Or it might be too small to support the next generation.

The newspapers in the Great Plains, most likely his home, do not run many help-wanted ads. The cowboy might have attended a community college for a while, but seldom has a university degree. He is not interested anyway in some nine-to-five job on an assembly line or behind a desk. He was born to be a cowboy. And inside the rodeo arena, if only for a handful of seconds, that's what he is.

He has memories of galloping across the open fields, of watching hawks circle over the barn at sunrise, of listening to the first bleat of a wet newborn calf in the crisp spring air. Now he lives in a town, most probably in a trailer, and breaks in a new saddle on the living room floor. But he clings to the hope that someday, if he wins enough prize money, he can buy a small herd of cattle, lease a patch of land, and spend his days trotting horseback across the scrub grass, somewhere at the end of the highway.

———

Unlike basketball or football, where a lack of height or muscle can relegate the ordinary young man to the sidelines, the rodeo cowboy comes in all sizes. Some of the toughest bull riders are so short they must strain to peer over the dashboard of a car. Bronc riders are usually slender, even downright skinny. Some steer wrestlers and calf ropers could accurately be called fat, although not prudently within earshot. But whatever the event, it is not the brawn of the cowboy that counts most, but the stoutness of his heart, or what rodeo cowboys call "try."

"He ain't got much talent," the saying goes, "but he's got a whole lot of try."

Women competed in rodeos with men until the 1930s, often riding masterfully. The most famous was "Prairie Rose" Henderson, who made her debut at the Cheyenne rodeo in 1901, against howls of resistance from the judges, and outshone most of the men for a share of the prize money. But after Bonnie McCarroll's bronc, Black Cat, fell over and killed her at the Pendleton rodeo in

1929, and Marie "Ma" Gibson died in a horse wreck in 1933, the rodeo promoters and fans grew queasy about the idea of the "fairer sex" courting such danger. Despite angry protests from the cowgirls, who noted that plenty of men had died in the arenas, women were banned from competition.

Today women are allowed to compete only in the barrel-racing event of the professional rodeo circuit. The announcers often lump them together in the same breath with the rodeo queens—"All the pretty girls of rodeo." But there is no primping or preening on the back of a racing horse.

———

During the early days of rodeo, the events were drawn directly from the work of the range cowboy: roping calves and riding broncs. Steer wrestling was added years later after Bill Pickett, a black cowboy with the famous 101 Ranch, bit a surprised steer on the lips during an exhibition and wrestled it to the ground.

Rodeo promoters have since introduced the spectacles of bareback bronc riding, bull riding, and barrel racing, where women on horseback speed around big drums laid out in a figure-eight pattern.

In the riding events, the cowboys and animals are judged separately, with equal weight for each, and the scores are added together for a possible total of 100 points. For the bronc, the higher the buck, the better the score. For the cowboy, points are awarded for bearing, control, and spurring action. The rider is scratched if he bucks off before eight seconds elapse. Under the rules, the cowboy must use only one hand to hold the rope, and the other hand must wave freely without touching any part of the animal. In the bronc-riding events, the spurs of the cowboy must rest above the shoulders of the horse as the ride begins, or he is disqualified.

The roping, wrestling, and barrel-racing events are based purely on time. The cowboy who can lasso a calf around the neck, flip it upside down, and tie three of its legs together in a knot of pigging string in the shortest time is the winner. In steer wrestling, each cowboy tries to be the fastest to seize the fleeing animal, slam it to the ground, and pin its horns to the turf. The winner of the barrel-racing contest is the cowgirl who can complete the pattern fastest. Knocking over a barrel brings a penalty of ten seconds, which invariably ruins any chance of placing in the money.

He's got a whole lot of try.

While each of the events claims some tie to the Old West, the real drama of rodeo, and the magnet for the crowds, is the riding of wild horses and angry bulls. The riders perform at one end of the arena, while the timed-event contestants work from the opposite end. But the two breeds of cowboy are separated by more than just 100 yards of dirt.

The biggest divide is bloodshed. Bull and bronc riders accept it as part of the bargain. Roping calves, on the other hand, might be tough on the animals but doesn't pose much of a threat to the cowboy.

The other big difference is money. The calf roper, steer wrestler, and barrel racer must own a horse, as well as a trailer to haul it. The investment can run $20,000 or more. But the bull or bronc rider needs only enough cash to get to the arena and pay his entry fees, since the mounts are furnished by the rodeo. Any young man with the dream, and the guts, can climb aboard. These cowboys are known as the "roughstock" men, and their lives are a constant struggle against biting the dust.

Hewey and the Wagon Cook

By Elmer Kelton

CHUCK-WAGON COOKS were expected to be contrary. It was part of their image, their defense mechanism against upstart young cowpunchers who might challenge their authority to rule their Dutch-oven kingdoms fifty or so feet in all directions from the chuck box. Woe unto the thoughtless cowboy who rode his horse within that perimeter and kicked up dust in the "kitchen."

The custom was so deeply ingrained that not even the owner of a ranch would easily violate this divine right of kings.

Even so, there were bounds, and Hewey Calloway was convinced that Dough-belly Jackson had stepped over the line. He considered Doughbelly a despot. Worse than that, Doughbelly was not even a very good cook. He never washed his hands until *after* he finished kneading dough for the biscuits, and he often failed to pick the rocks out of his beans before he cooked them. Some of the hands said they could live with that because the rocks were occasionally softer than Doughbelly's beans anyway, and certainly softer than his biscuits.

What stuck worst in Hewey's craw, though, was Doughbelly's unnatural fondness for canned tomatoes. They went into just about everything he cooked except the coffee.

"If it wasn't for them tomatoes, he couldn't cook a lick," Hewey complained to fellow puncher Grady Welch. "If Ol' C. C. Tarpley had to eat after Doughbelly for three or four days runnin', he'd fire him."

C. C. Tarpley's West Texas ranch holdings were spread for a considerable distance on both sides of the Pecos River, from the sandhills to the greasewood hard-lands. They were so large that he had to keep two wagons and two roundup crews on the range at one time. Grady pointed out, "He knows. That's why he spends most all his time with the other wagon. Reason he hired Doughbelly is that he can get him for ten dollars a month cheaper than any other cook workin' out of Midland. Old C. C. is frugal."

Frugal did not seem a strong enough word. Hewey said, "Tight, is what I'd call it."

Doughbelly was by all odds the worst belly-robber it had been Hewey's misfortune to know, and Hewey had been punching cattle on one outfit or another since he was thirteen or fourteen. He had had his thirtieth birthday last February, though it was four or five days afterward that he first thought about it. It didn't matter; Doughbelly wouldn't have baked him a cake anyway. The lazy reprobate couldn't even make a decent cobbler pie if he had a washtub full of dried apples. Not that Old C. C. was likely to buy any such apples in the first place. C. C. was, as Hewey said, tight.

Grady was limping, the result of being thrown twice from a jug-headed young bronc. He said, "You ought to feel a little sympathy for Doughbelly. He ain't got a ridin' job like us."

"He gets paid more than we do."

Grady rubbed a skinned hand across a dark bruise and lacerations on the left side of his face, a present from two cows that had knocked him down and trampled him. "But he don't have near as much fun as us."

"I just think he ought to earn his extra pay, that's all."

Grady warned, "Was I you, I'd be careful what I said where Doughbelly could hear me. Ringy as he is, he might throw his apron at you and tell you to do the cookin' yourself."

It wasn't that Hewey couldn't cook. He had done his share of line-camp batching, one place and another. He could throw together some pretty nice fixings, even if he said so himself. He just didn't fancy wrestling pots and pans. It was not a job a man could do a-horseback. Hewey had hired on to cowboy.

He appreciated payday like any cowpuncher, though money was not his first consideration. He had once quit a forty-dollar-a-month job to take one that paid just thirty. The difference was that the lower-paying outfit had a cook who could make red beans taste like ambrosia. A paycheck might not last more

Chuck-wagon cooks were expected to be contrary.

than a few hours in town, or anyway a long night, but good chuck was to be enjoyed day after day.

Hewey was tempted to draw his time and put a lot of miles between him and Doughbelly Jackson, but he was bound to the Two C's by an old cowboy ethic, an unwritten rule. It was that you don't quit an outfit in the middle of the works and leave it short-handed. That would increase the burden of labor on friends like Grady Welch. He and Grady had known each other since they were shirttail buttons, working their way up from horse jingler to top hand. They had made a trip up the trail to Kansas together once, and they had shared the same cell in jail after a trail-end celebration that got a little too loud for the locals.

Grady was a good old boy, and it wouldn't be fair to ride off and leave him to pick up the slack. Hewey had made up his mind to stick until the works were done or he died of tomato poisoning, whichever came first.

It was the canned tomatoes that caused Doughbelly's first real blowup. Hewey found them mixed in the beans once too often and casually remarked that someday he was going to buy himself a couple of tomatoes and start riding, and he would keep riding until he reached a place where somebody asked him what to call that fruit he was carrying on his saddle.

"That's where I'll spend the rest of my days, where nobody knows what a tomato is," he said.

For some reason Hewey couldn't quite understand, Doughbelly seemed to take umbrage at that remark. He ranted at length about ignorant cowboys who didn't know fine cuisine when they tasted it. He proceeded to burn both the biscuits and the beans for the next three days. Another thing Hewey didn't quite understand was that the rest of the cowboys seemed to blame him instead of Doughbelly. Even Grady Welch, good compadre that he was, stayed a little cool toward Hewey until Doughbelly got back into a fair-to-middling humor.

After three days of culinary torture, those tomatoes didn't taste so bad to the rest of the hands. For Hewey, though, they had not improved a bit.

Like most outfits, the Two C's had two wagons for each camp. The chuck wagon was the most important, for it had the chuck box from which the cook operated, and it carried most of the foodstuffs like the flour and coffee, lard and sugar, and whatever canned goods the ranch owner would consent to pay for. The second, known as the hoodlum wagon, carried cowboy bedrolls, the branding irons, and other necessities. It also had a dried cowhide, known as a cooney, slung beneath its bed for collection of good dry firewood wherever it might be found along the way between camps.

Like most of the cowhands, cow boss Matthew Mullins was a little down on Hewey for getting the cook upset and causing three days' meals to be spoiled. So when it came time to move camp to the Red Mill pasture, he singled Hewey out for the least desirable job the outfit offered: helping Doughbelly load up, then driving the hoodlum wagon. Hewey bristled a little, though on reflection he decided it had been worth it all to dig Doughbelly in his well-padded ribs about those cussed tomatoes.

The rest of the hands left camp, driving the remuda in front of them. Doughbelly retired to his blankets, spread in the thin shade of a large and aged mesquite tree, to take himself a little siesta before he and Hewey hitched the teams. A little peeved at being left with all the dirty work, Hewey loaded the utensils and pitched the cowboys' bedrolls up into the hoodlum wagon. He could hear Doughbelly still snoring. He decided to steal a few minutes' shut-eye himself beneath one of the wagons.

The cowhide cooney sagged low beneath the hoodlum wagon, so Hewey crawled under the chuck wagon. His lingering resentment would not let him sleep. He lay staring up at the bottom of the wagon bed. Dry weather had shrunk the boards enough that there was a little space between them. He could see the rims of several cans.

Gradually it dawned on him that those cans held the tomatoes he had come to hate so much. And with that realization came a notion so deliciously wicked that he began laughing to himself. He took a jackknife from his pocket and opened the largest blade, testing the point of it on his thumb.

Hewey did not have much in the way of worldly possessions, but he took care of what he had. He had always been particular about keeping his knife sharp as a razor. A man never knew when he might find something that needed cutting. He poked the blade between the boards, made contact with the bottom of a can, then drove the knife upward.

The can resisted, and Hewey was afraid if he pushed any harder he might break the blade. He climbed out from beneath the wagon and quietly opened the chuck box. From a drawer he extracted Doughbelly's heavy butcher knife and carried it back underneath. He slipped it between the boards, then pushed hard.

The sound of rending metal was loud, and he feared it might be enough to awaken Doughbelly. He paused to listen. He still heard the cook's snoring. He began moving around beneath the wagon, avoiding the streaming tomato juice as he punched can after can. When one stream turned out to be molasses, he decided he had finished the tomatoes, at least all he could reach. He wiped the blade on dry grass, then on his trousers, and put the knife back into the chuck box.

Whistling a happy church tune he had learned at a brush-arbor camp meeting, he went abut harnessing the two teams.

Doughbelly rolled his bedding, grousing all the while about some people being too joyful for their own good. Concerned that the cook might notice the leaking tomatoes and the molasses, Hewey hitched the team to the wagon for him while Doughbelly went off behind the bushes and took care of other business. He had both wagons ready to go when the cook came back.

He had to fight himself to keep from grinning like a cat stealing cream. Doughbelly stared suspiciously at him before climbing up onto the seat of the chuck wagon. "Don't you lag behind and make me have to wait for you to open the gates."

Opening gates for the wagon cook was almost as lowly a job as chopping wood and helping wash the cookware, but today Hewey did not mind. "I'll stick close behind you."

For a while, following in the chuck-wagon's tracks, Hewey could see thin lines of glistening wetness where the tomato juice and molasses strung along in the grass. The lines stopped when the cans had emptied.

Hewey rejoiced, and sang all the church songs he could remember.

As he walked past the chuck wagon to open a wire gate for Doughbelly, the cook commented, "I never knowed you was a religious sort."

"Sing a glad song and the angels sing with you."

Hewey knew there would sooner or later be hell to pay, but he had never been inclined to worry much about future consequences if what he did felt right at the time.

He helped Doughbelly set up camp, unhitching the teams, pitching the bedrolls to the ground, digging a fire pit, and chopping up dry mesquite. Doughbelly mostly stood around with ham-sized hands on his hips and giving unnecessary directions. The cowboys came straggling in after putting the remuda in a large fenced trap for the night. They were to brand calves here tomorrow, then move camp again in the afternoon.

Hewey had never been able to keep a secret from Grady Welch. They had spent so much time working together that Grady seemed able to read his mind. He gave Hewey a quizzical look and said, "You been up to somethin'."

Hewey put on the most innocent air he could muster. "I'm ashamed of you. Never saw anybody with such a suspicious mind."

"If you've done somethin' to cause us three more days of burned biscuits, the boys'll run you plum out of camp."

The camp was thirty miles from Upton City, and even that was not much of a town.

"All I done was dull ol' Cookie's butcher knife a little."

Doughbelly started fixing supper. Hewey tried to watch him from the corner of his eye without being obvious. He held his breath when the cook reached over the sideboards and lifted out a can. Doughbelly's mouth dropped open. He gave the can a shake and exclaimed, "That thievin' grocery store has swindled the company."

He flung the can aside and fetched another, with the same result. This time he felt wetness on his hand and turned the can over. His eyes widened as he saw the hole punched in the bottom. "How in the Billy Hell . . ."

He whipped his gaze to Hewey. He seemed to sense instantly that Hewey Calloway was the agent of his distress. He drew back his arm and hurled the can at Hewey's head. Hewey ducked, then turned and began to pull away as Doughbelly picked up a chunk of firewood and ran at him.

"Damn you, Hewey, I don't know how you done it, but I know you done it."

The other cowboys moved quickly out of the way as Hewey broke into a run through bear grass and sand. The soft-bellied cook heaved along in his wake, waving the heavy stick of firewood and shouting words that would cause every church in Midland to bar him for life.

Cow boss Matthew Mullins rode up in time to see the cook stumble in a patch of shinnery and flop on his stomach. Like Doughbelly, he instantly blamed Hewey for whatever had gone wrong. "Hewey Calloway, what shenanigan have you run this time?"

Any show of innocence would be lost on Mullins. Hewey did not even try. "I just saved us from havin' to eat all them canned tomatoes."

"You probably kept us from eatin' *anything*. It'll be a week before he cooks chuck fit to put in our mouths."

"He ain't cooked anything yet that was fit to eat."

Mullins motioned for Hewey to remain where he was, a fit distance from the chuck wagon, while the boss went over to try to soothe the cook's wounded dignity. Watching from afar, Hewey could not hear the words, but he could see the violent motions Doughbelly was making with his hands, and he imagined he could even see the red that flushed the cook's face.

By the slump in Mullins's shoulders, Hewey discerned that the pleadings had come to naught. Doughbelly stalked over to the chuck wagon and dragged his bedroll through the sand, far away from those belonging to the rest of the crew. His angry voice would have carried a quarter mile.

"By God," he declared, "I quit!"

Mullins trailed after him, pleading. If he had been a dog, his tail would have been between his legs. "But you can't quit in the middle of the works. There's supper to be fixed and hands to be fed."

Doughbelly dropped his bedroll fifty feet from the wagon and plopped his broad butt down upon it. "They can feed theirselves or do without. I quit!"

Hewey had roped many a runaway cow and dragged her back into the roundup, bawling and fighting her head. He knew the signs of a sull when he saw them, and he saw them now in Doughbelly.

Mullins stared at the cook for a minute, but it was obvious he had run out of argument. He turned and approached Hewey with a firm stride that said it was a good thing he did not have a rope in his hand. His voice crackled. "Hewey, you've raised hell and shoved a chunk under it."

Hewey felt a little like laughing, but he knew better than to show it. "I didn't do nothin', and anyway the old scudder had it comin'."

"You know he'll sit out there and sulk like a baby. He won't cook a lick of supper."

"I've heard a lot worse news than that."

"You ain't heard the worst yet. Since he won't cook, you're goin' to."

"I ain't paid to cook."

"You'll cook or you'll start out walkin'. It's thirty miles to Upton City and farther than that to Midland. Which'll it be?"

Thirty miles, carrying saddle and bedroll . . . For a cowboy, used to saddling a horse rather than walk a hundred yards, that was worse than being sentenced to sixty days in jail. He looked at Doughbelly. "Maybe if I went and apologized to him . . ." He did not finish, because he had rather walk than apologize for doing what every man in the outfit would like to have done.

Mullins said, "You're either cookin' or walkin'."

Hewey swallowed. "Damn, but this is a hard outfit to work for." But he turned toward the chuck wagon. "I've never cooked for anybody except myself, hardly."

"Nothin' to it. You just fix what you'd fix for yourself and multiply it by twelve. And it had better be fit to eat."

"At least there won't be no tomatoes in it."

Hewey had always taken pride in two distinctions: He had never picked cotton, and he had never herded sheep. He had not considered the possibility that he might someday cook at a wagon or he might have added that as a third item on the list. Now he would never be able to.

He grumbled to himself as he sliced the beef and made biscuit dough and set the coffeepot over the fire. He glared at the distant form of Doughbelly Jackson squatted on his bedroll, his back turned toward the wagon. He figured hunger would probably put the old scoundrel in a better frame of mind when supper was ready, and he would come back into camp as if nothing had happened. But he had not reckoned on how obstinate a wagon cook could be when he got a sure-enough case of the rings.

At last Hewey hollered, "Chuck," and the cowboys filed by the chuck box for their utensils, then visited the pots and Dutch ovens. He fully expected to hear some complaints when they bit into his biscuits, but nobody had any adverse comments. They were probably all afraid the cooking chore might fall on them if they said anything.

Grady Welch tore a high-rise biscuit in two and took a healthy bite. His eyes registered momentary surprise. "Kind of salty," he said, then quickly added, "and that's just the way I like them."

Hewey looked toward Doughbelly. He still sat where he had been for more than an hour, his back turned. Matthew Mullins edged up to Hewey. "Seein' as you're the one caused all this, maybe you ought to take him somethin' to eat."

"The only thing wrong with him is his head. Ain't nothin' wrong with his legs."

"At least take him a cup of coffee."

Hewey thought a little about that thirty-mile walk and poured steaming black coffee into a tin cup. Each leg felt as if it weighed a hundred pounds as he made his reluctant way out to the bedroll where Doughbelly had chosen to make his stand, sitting down. He extended the cup toward the cook. "Here. Boss said you'd ought to take some nourishment."

To his surprise, Doughbelly accepted the cup. He stared up at Hewey, his eyes smoldering like barbecue coals, then tossed the coffee out into the grass. He pitched the cup at Hewey. "Go to hell!"

"I feel like I'm already halfway there." Hewey's foot itched. He was sorely tempted to place it where it might do the most good, but he managed to put down his baser instincts. He picked up the cup. "Then sit here and pout. You're missin' a damned good supper."

Hewey knew it wasn't all that good, but he guessed Doughbelly would sober up if he thought somebody else might have taken his place and be doing a better job.

That turned out to be another bad guess. Doughbelly never came to supper. At dark he rolled out his bedding and turned in. Hewey sat in lantern light and picked rocks out of the beans he would slow-cook through the night.

Mullins came up and lifted Doughbelly's alarm clock from the chuck box. "You'd better put this by your bed tonight. If he don't get up at four o'clock in the mornin', it'll be your place to crawl out and fix breakfast."

Hewey felt that he could probably throw the clock fifty feet and strike Doughbelly squarely on the head. He took pleasure in the fantasy but said only, "If I have to."

As Mullins walked away, Grady sidled up. "He's bound to get hungry and come in."

Hewey glumly shook his head. "He could live off of his own lard for two weeks."

Hewey lay half awake a long time, then drifted off into a dream in which he fought his way out from a huge vat of clinging biscuit dough, only to fall into an even bigger can of tomatoes. The ringing of the alarm saved him from drowning in the juice. He arose and pulled on his trousers and boots, then punched up the banked coals and coaxed the fire back into full life. He kept watching for Doughbelly to come into camp, but the cook remained far beyond the firelight.

After a time Hewey shook the kid horse jingler out of a deep sleep and sent him off to bring in the remuda so the cowboys could catch out their mounts after breakfast. He entertained a wild notion of intercepting the horses and turning them in such a way that they would run over the cook's bed, but he had to dismiss the idea. The laws against murder made no special dispensation for wagon cooks.

The cowboys saddled up, a couple of broncs pitching, working off the friskiness brought on by the fresh morning air. Grady Welch had to grab the saddle horn to stay aboard. Pride gave way to practicality; he was still aching from the last time when he *didn't* claw leather. Hewey had to stand beside the chuck box and watch the cowboys ride out from camp without him. He felt low enough to walk beneath the wagon without bending over.

Doughbelly rolled his blankets, then sat there just as he had done yesterday, shoulders hunched and back turned. Hewey went out to a pile of well-dried wood a Two C's swamper had cut last winter for this campsite. He began chopping it into short lengths for the cook-fire.

He heard the rattle of a lid and turned in time to see Doughbelly at the Dutch ovens, filling a plate. Hewey hurled a chunk of wood at him. Doughbelly retreated to his bedroll and sat there eating. Angrily Hewey dumped the leftover breakfast onto the ground and raked it into the sand with a pot hook to be sure Doughbelly could not come back for a second helping. He hid a couple of biscuits for the kid horse jingler, who would come in hungry about midmorning.

Hewey was resigned to cooking the noon meal, for Doughbelly showed no sign that he was ready to come to terms. He peeled spuds and ground fresh coffee and sliced steaks from half a beef that had been wrapped in a tarp and hung up in the nearby windmill tower to keep it from the flies and larger varmints.

From afar he glumly watched horsemen bring the cattle into the pens, cut the calves off from their mothers, and start branding them. He belonged out there with the rest of the hands, not here confined to a few feet on either side of the chuck box. He had been in jails where he felt freer.

Doughbelly still sat where he had been since suppertime, ignoring everything that went on around him.

The hands came in for dinner, then went back to complete the branding. Finished, they brought the irons and put them in the hoodlum wagon. Mullins told Hewey, "The boys'll drive the horses to the next camp, so the jingler'll be free to drive the hoodlum wagon for you."

By that Hewey knew he was still stuck with the cooking job. He jerked his head toward Doughbelly. "What about him?"

Mullins shrugged. "He's your problem." He mounted a dun horse and rode off.

The kid helped Hewey finish loading the two wagons and hitch the teams. Hewey checked to be sure he had secured the chuck-box lid so it would not drop if a wheel hit a bad bump.

At last Doughbelly stood up. He stretched himself, taking his time, then picked up his bedroll and carried it to the hoodlum wagon. He pitched it up on top of the other hands' bedding.

An old spiritual tune ran through Hewey's mind, and he began to sing. "Just a closer walk with Thee . . ."

He climbed up on the hoodlum wagon, past the surprised kid, and threw Doughbelly's bedroll back onto the ground.

Doughbelly sputtered. "Hey, what're you doin'?"

Hewey pointed in the direction of Upton City. "It ain't but thirty miles. If you step lively you might make it by tomorrow night."

He returned to the chuck wagon and took his place on the seat, then flipped the reins. The team surged against the harness. He sang, "As I walk, let me walk close to Thee."

Doughbelly trotted alongside, his pudgy face red, his eyes wide in alarm. "You can't just leave me here."

"You ain't workin' for this outfit. You quit yesterday."

"Hewey . . ." Doughbelly's voice trailed off. He trotted back to where his bedroll lay. He lifted it up onto his shoulder and came running. Hewey was surprised to see that a man with that big a belly on him could run so fast. He had never seen the cook move like that before.

Hewey put the team into a long trot, one that Doughbelly could not match. The kid followed Hewey's cue and set the hoodlum wagon to moving too fast for the cook to catch.

Hewey had to give the man credit; he tried. Doughbelly pushed himself hard, but he could not help falling back. At last he stumbled, and the bed came undone, tarp and blankets rolling out upon the grass. Doughbelly sank to the ground, a picture of hopelessness.

Hewey let the team go a little farther, then hauled up on the lines. He signaled the kid to circle around him and go on. Then he sat and waited. Doughbelly gathered his blankets in a haphazard manner, picking up the rope that had held them but not taking time to tie it. He came on, puffing like a T&P locomotive. By the time he finally reached the wagon, he was so winded he could hardly speak. Sweat cut muddy trails through the dust on his ruddy face.

"Please, Hewey, ain't you goin' to let me throw my beddin' up there?"

Hewey gave him his most solemn expression. "If you ain't cookin', you ain't ridin'."

"I'm cookin'."

"What about them damned tomatoes?"

"Never really liked them much myself."

Hewey moved over to the left side of the wagon seat and held out the reins. "Long's you're workin' for this outfit again, you'd just as well do the drivin'. I'm goin' to sit back and take my rest."

Supper that night was the best meal Hewey had eaten since Christmas.

From *Breaking Clean*

By Judy Blunt

AT THREE, THE BLIZZARD HITS like a freight train. . . . When it hit, the house bent
and shrieked, a sound like nails pulled from damp wood. In the bedroom on
the northwest corner of the house, my father woke, his breath visible in the air
over his head. Cold enough to freeze pipes. He turned on the light long enough
to find his jeans and socks. The window on the north wall rattled steadily, the
curtains trembling, panes plastered with snow. The stove in the living room ran
on fuel oil, #2 diesel, but there were no thermostats to kick on when the temperature dropped. In the dark, he made his way to the kitchen to hit the overhead light switch, then back to the oil heater. He turned the dial to "high" and
pawed the litter of mittens and boots to one side. High meant cherry-red. The
stove in the kitchen ran on cottonwood, a couple of logs ready on the floor
beside it, a couple of days' worth stacked in the porch. He fed fires, turned on
faucets, opened bedroom doors, made the necessary rounds with tense efficiency. The noise seemed impossible. Stovepipes hummed, beams creaked, snow
blasted against the north windows like birdshot. Overriding it all was the wind,
an urgent moaning under the eaves that rose in sustained shrieks, like a catfight.

He turned off the light, leaned over the cookstove, and rested a hand
against the kitchen window, trying to see movement in the wall of solid gray
outside. Was the house drifted under? The frigid draft leaking through the
frame said not, but there was no light, no shape of trees by the house, no way
to judge the speed of the blowing snow. The illusion was one of stillness, a dark
blanket held up to the glass. The window looked south, toward the feed ground,
the stack yard. He stood a moment with the sound of the storm settling in his

gut, trying to imagine his cows huddled against the fence, sheltered by the long row of haystacks. He might get them into the lot by the barn. He reached for the coffeepot, lifted the basket of used grounds, then stopped and leaned against the stove again. The wind was all wrong, north and west. The cattle were gone. He found his way back to bed in the dark. My mother's voice lifted in a question, and he answered her, "tougher than hell out there." He lay back, listening to the roar. Nothing he could do until daylight.

As what passed for dawn approached, only the prairie birds and children slept on unaware of the storm. Inside our house nine people curled closer to bedmates, drawing quilts over their noses against the chill. The boys had camped out on the living room floor, their bed given over to Granddad, our mother's father. Two neighbor girls were crowded into the cot-sized bunk beds with Gail and me, stranded at our house since school let out the day before. Their mom had buried her pickup in a drift trying to get them and had to dig out and turn back.

My parents rose early, before true light. The smells of bacon and coffee and backdraft smoke drifted through the house, sharpened by the nip of frost. Cold radiated from the bedrooms where the outside walls sandwiched a thin insulation of tar paper, old newspapers, and Depression-era *Saturday Evening Posts,* and the household gathered as it woke, driven toward the roar of the woodstove. Outside the windows, the air turned white as the sun rose, lighter but no less dense, no quieter. Breakfast occurred in shifts as places cleared at the table, adults tense, preoccupied, children hushed with excitement. As we planned our unexpected vacation from school, Dad dressed for morning chores in layers of long johns, coveralls, lined buckskin mitts, his cap pulled low over his eyes, earflaps secured by a wool scarf. Another scarf covered the back of his neck, a third wrapped the bottom of his face. He tucked his coveralls into the tops of his overshoes and buckled them down, finishing as Mom filled the milk pail with hot water for the chickens.

The barn lay a hundred yards south of the house, the low, red granary and chicken house a bit west of there, all of it lost in blowing snow. Stepping away from the porch, Dad aimed east for the yard gate, and then south, guided by the built-in compass of a man who has walked the same path at least twice a day for ten years. A big man, over six feet tall, over two hundred pounds, centered in his chest and shoulders, and still it was difficult to stay grounded. The wind cut through the back of his coat as he braced against the storm and

Coming home meant walking into the storm.

fought to keep his feet in the unfamiliar sea of hard drifts, digging in with his heels at every step.

The chickens met the cold by roosting with their feet drawn up, their feathers fluffed like chickadees. Dad fed them, poured water in their bucket. He left the eggs in one nest, their shells split lengthwise, the frozen whites bulging through like scar tissue. The milk cow, a thin-skinned Guernsey/Angus cross, could stay in the barn until the storm let up, he decided. The lack of water wouldn't kill her for one day. She was almost dry anyway, set to calve in March. The feeder calves would be huddled in the open-faced shed, safer there than if he tried to lure them out for grain. He saw no sign of the range cows. He could do no more.

Coming home meant walking into the storm, and within minutes his compass failed in the face of the wind. Eyes slitted against the stab of ice crystals, he breathed in shallow grunts, his airway clamping down as it would for a draft of pure ammonia. He couldn't get enough air. Every few yards, he swung his back to the blizzard and stopped to catch his breath, then turned into it again, walking blind for what seemed like too long. He corrected to the right and back to the left, trying to find northwest by feel, knowing he might have passed arm's length from the yard fence without seeing it. Sweat chilled on his ribs. A few more minutes and he would let the wind carry him south again. The windbreak or corrals would stop him and guide him back to the barn.

As he blundered left a last time, a single strand of No. 9 wire caught him across the chest and sprang him back in his tracks. He'd stumbled into the clothesline. He was halfway home. Keeping the wire in his left mitt, he bent his head into the wind and followed it until the end of the old house trailer, our bunkhouse, loomed out of white air in front of him. From there, another giant step west to the yard fence, the woven wire buried halfway to the top. Downwind from the house, he stopped a last time to strain air through a cupped mitten, then walked toward the light in the kitchen window.

Mom took the pail from his hand and set it hissing on the woodstove to thaw out. The milk had slopped up and stuck to the sides, coating the inside with a thick rime, white ice on stainless steel. Above the scarf, Dad's face had turned the same blue-gray shade. The headgear had frozen together and came off in one piece. Under the scarf, the skin had stiffened in deep furrows that reddened quickly in the heat of the kitchen. I watched him as he thawed out, ice dripping from lashes and brows, his lips limbering to sip coffee. But his cheeks stayed rigid for a long time, stuck in a grimace or a scream. Over the course of the afternoon, the welts softened into frown lines as he passed from window to window, stepping around the card table where Granddad tried to keep us settled to a game of pinochle. They reappeared as he bared his teeth and squinted through the glass into the storm. We stayed out of his way.

Mom rattled pots and peeled potatoes, working at the logistics of three meals, nine mouths, descending with swift justice whenever our quarrels overrode the drone of the wind. Cramped up in the living room to stay warm, we six children grew quickly tired of cards, tired of board games, tired of each other. As a last resort, she hauled boxes of ornaments from their hiding spot and let us squabble over decorating the Christmas tree we'd hauled from the Breaks over the weekend. When the water pipes froze in the middle of the day, Dad grabbed the torch and headed for the basement like a man bent on tunneling out of prison.

That evening, he kept to his place at the table, drinking more coffee, feeding the woodstove, while Mom worked after supper. Their voices circled the kitchen, undercurrents of worry. The cattle were now more than twenty-four hours from their last full stomach, their last drink of water. They were heading into their second night of trying to breathe in the god-awful wind, their metabolism kicked into full gear, burning on high like the fuel-oil stove. When the tanks ran dry, then what? My parents knew. . . .

———

The wind battered through the afternoon and into the night, and we rose the second morning nearly immune to it, voices pitched a notch louder to be heard over the steady scream. Midmorning, the air brightened and the gray shadow of cottonwood trunks appeared outside the kitchen window, then the fence posts further out. By noon, we could see the blurred outlines of the barn and outbuildings. Our voices rang loud in our own ears. In another hour the wind lifted and was gone like a curtain rising on an empty stage. Outside, the temperature held at a crystal thirty-five degrees below zero. Nothing moved in the silence. Nothing showed above the hazy peaks of snow, no horizon appeared where the transformed landscape met the sky under a white December sun.

Dad organized with the urgency of someone held down too long. The shop door, a wide steel panel hung on rollers, had to be shoveled free to get the four-wheel-drive pickup. He picked his way around the worst of it getting to the stackyard for hay, but where the gates had plugged bumper-deep, he hacked the drifts with a spade, breaking the solid pack into chunks he could lift to one side with the bigger scoop shovel. The haystacks had made a perfect snow fence, capturing ten feet of snow on the downwind side, so he shoveled and floundered his way to the upwind side. The pitchfork crunched into the stack. In later years he would have a tractor with a hydraulic grapple fork, and perhaps those huge steel jaws could have taken a bite from the north side of the stack. But the wind had pounded snow so deeply into the hay and frozen it so solidly that one man heaving at a pitchfork could not free a wisp of it. It would take all day to shovel in from the drifted side. Climbing a stack of small square bales, he wrenched a few free and loosed them like toboggans down the steep slope toward the pickup.

Sound carries for miles in still air. He stood atop the stack and looked south, calling his cows, listening for the answering bawl. Silence snapped shut behind his voice. The winter pasture is relatively small, half a mile wide and a mile long, really more of a holding pasture than a grazing pasture, but rolling hills hide the south half from view. The county road borders the east fence line, and from the stack he could see the darker stripe of the raised grade, blown clear in some spots, covered in others.

Mom and twelve-year-old Kenny were bundled and waiting when he pulled up at the house, and they struck off for the county lane. Low drifts held the weight of the pickup; the deep ones tapering toward the ditch could be avoided. Within minutes they spotted the first of them, four cows pressed against the east fence, just across the ditch. All four were down and drifted over, two dead and frozen stiff, the other two only half dead, unable to rise. They grabbed shovels to scoop the snow pack away from their heads, broke a bale and tucked squares of hay within reach, temporary measures. A minute later, they piled back in the pickup, fueled by a new sense of urgency.

Topping a low rise, the pickup slowed as the herd came into view. The cab was silent except for the warm blast of the defroster against the windshield. The fence corner was drifted full. One cow hung dead near the corner post, her hind legs twisted in the brace wires where she had walked up a drift and fallen through over the fence line. A few had made it out, pushing forward and stepping over the bodies of cows that had fallen and been buried against the wire. Some stood belly-deep in the ditch, others on the road. One had floundered on across, walking with the wind until her front feet slipped through the grate of a cattle guard. She had frozen standing up, still heading southeast. Forty head were still alive, the bulk of them gathered in the vee of the fence corner. . . .

Snow had frozen a crust across each back, down each side, smoothing away evidence of the dark hair beneath. Pounds of ice sheathed their heads and hung in cones from their noses to the ground, breath grown solid in the bitter cold. What scant air they could draw whistled and puffed from slim vent holes half a foot from the tips of their noses. It was the only noise the cows made as Dad walked among them, struggling to find his own, some feature he recognized under the white cast. They stood motionless, though his steps creaked and squawked against the snow inches from their lowered heads. Eyes sealed tight under an inch of milky ice, they waited, blind and dumb, rigid with shock.

There was, he would say later, nothing to be done but what they did, an act both vicious and loving, desperate and calm. Pain, their pain, his pain, had reached the cold plateau that allows no more. The cattle couldn't hurt any worse. He could no longer do nothing. Raising the pliers in a wide arc, he swung them flat across a cow's face, shattering the ice that sealed her eyes, again across the bridge of her nose. Now there was motion, noise, as the animals fought to escape the crack of steel against their heads, grunting as their nostrils broke free and air rushed into their lungs. Mom stepped across the ditch where the fence was opened, a piece of board she had wrenched from the pickup bed clenched in both hands. Together they moved through the herd, the forty head of cows and both bulls still alive, and beat away the ice that was killing them, battering against the shields until the eyes jarred open, and again, until the whites rolled in fear and tongues hung from gaping mouths, until the cows began to struggle and live.

The Reformation of Calliope

By O. Henry

CALLIOPE CATESBY was in his humors again. Ennui was upon him. This goodly promontory, the earth—particularly that portion of it known as Quicksand—was to him no more than a pestilent congregation of vapors. Overtaken by the megrims, the philosopher may seek relief in soliloquy; my lady find solace in tears; the flaccid Easterner scold at the millinery bills of his women folk. Such recourse was insufficient to the denizens of Quicksand. Calliope, especially, was wont to express his ennui according to his lights.

Overnight, Calliope had hung out signals of approaching low spirits. He had kicked his own dog on the porch of the Occidental Hotel and refused to apologize. He had become capricious and faultfinding in conversation. While strolling about he reached often for twigs of mesquite and chewed the leaves fiercely. That was always an ominous act. Another symptom alarming to those who were familiar with the different stages of his doldrums was his increasing politeness and a tendency to use formal phrases. A husky softness succeeded the usual penetrating drawl in his tones. A dangerous courtesy marked his manners. Later, his smile became crooked, the left side of his mouth slanting upward, and Quicksand got ready to stand from under.

At this stage Calliope generally began to drink. Finally, about midnight, he was seen going homeward, saluting those whom he met with exaggerated but inoffensive courtesy. Not yet was Calliope's melancholy at the danger point. He would seat himself at the window of the room he occupied over Silvester's tonsorial parlor and there chant lugubrious and tuneless ballads until morning, accompanying the noises by appropriate maltreatment of a jangling guitar. More magnanimous than Nero, he would thus give musical warning of the forthcoming municipal upheaval that Quicksand was scheduled to endure.

A quiet, amiable man was Calliope Catesby at other times—quiet to indolence and amiable to worthlessness. At best he was a loafer and a nuisance; at worst he was the Terror of Quicksand. His ostensible occupation was something subordinate in the real estate line; he drove the beguiled Easterner in buckboards out to look over lots and ranch property. Originally he came from one of the Gulf States, his lank six feet, slurring rhythm of speech, and sectional idioms giving evidence of his birthplace.

And yet, after taking on Western adjustments, this languid pine-box whittler, cracker-barrel hugger, shady corner lounger of the cotton fields and sumac hills of the South became famed as a bad man among men who had made a lifelong study of the art of truculence.

At nine the next morning, Calliope was fit. Inspired by his own barbarous melodies and the contents of his jug, he was ready primed to gather fresh laurels from the diffident brow of Quicksand. Encircled and crisscrossed with cartridge belts, abundantly garnished with revolvers, and copiously drunk, he poured forth into Quicksand's main street. Too chivalrous to surprise and capture a town by silent sortie, he paused at the nearest corner and emitted his slogan—that fearful, brassy yell, so reminiscent of the steam piano, that had gained for him the classic appellation that had superseded his own baptismal name. Following close upon his vociferation came three shots from his forty-five by way of limbering up the guns and testing his aim. A yellow dog, the personal property of Colonel Swazey, the proprietor of the Occidental, fell feet upward in the dust with one farewell yelp. A Mexican who was crossing the street from the Blue Front grocery, carrying in his hand a bottle of kerosene, was stimulated to a sudden and admirable burst of speed, still grasping the neck of the shattered bottle. The new gilt weathercock on Judge Riley's lemon and ultramarine two-story residence shivered, flapped, and hung by a splinter, the sport of the wanton breezes.

The artillery was in trim. Calliope's hand was steady. The high, calm ecstasy of habitual battle was upon him, though slightly embittered by the sadness of Alexander in that his conquests were limited to the small world of Quicksand.

Calliope Catesby made a lifelong study of the art of truculence.

Down the street went Calliope, shooting right and left. Glass fell like hail; dogs vamoosed; chickens flew, squawking; feminine voices shrieked concernedly to youngsters at large. The din was perforated at intervals by the *staccato* of the Terror's guns, and was drowned periodically by the brazen screech that Quicksand knew so well. The occasions of Calliope's low spirits were legal holidays in Quicksand. All along the main street, in advance of his coming, clerks were putting up shutters and closing doors. Business would languish for a space. The right of way was Calliope's, and as he advanced, observing the dearth of opposition and the few opportunities for distraction, his ennui perceptibly increased.

But some four squares farther down, lively preparations were being made to minister to Mr. Catesby's love for interchange of compliments and repartee. On the previous night, numerous messengers had hastened to advise Buck Patterson, the city marshal, of Calliope's impending eruption. The patience of that official, often strained in extending leniency toward the disturber's misdeeds, had been overtaxed. In Quicksand some indulgence was accorded the natural ebullition of human nature. Providing that the lives of the more useful citizens were not recklessly squandered, or too much property needlessly laid waste, the community sentiment was against a too strict enforcement of the law. But Calliope had raised the limit. His outbursts had been too frequent and too violent to come within the classification of a normal and sanitary relaxation of spirit.

Buck Patterson had been expecting and awaiting in his little ten-by-twelve frame office that preliminary yell announcing that Calliope was feeling blue. When the signal came, the city marshal rose to his feet and buckled on his guns. Two deputy sheriffs and three citizens who had proven the edible qualities of fire also stood up, ready to bandy with Calliope's leaden jocularities.

"Gather that fellow in," said Buck Patterson, setting forth the lines of the campaign. "Don't have no talk, but shoot as soon as you can get a show. Keep behind cover and bring him down. He's a nogood 'un. It's up to Calliope to turn up his toes this time, I reckon. Go to him all spraddled out, boys. And don't git too reckless, for what Calliope shoots at he hits."

Buck Patterson, tall, muscular, and solemn-faced, with his bright "City Marshal" badge shining on the breast of his blue flannel shirt, gave his posse directions for the onslaught upon Calliope. The plan was to accomplish the downfall of the Quicksand Terror without loss to the attacking party, if possible.

The splenetic Calliope, unconscious of retributive plots, was steaming down the channel, cannonading on either side, when he suddenly became aware of breakers ahead. The city marshal and one of the deputies rose up behind some dry-goods boxes half a square to the front and opened fire. At the same time the rest of the posse, divided, shelled him from two side streets up which they were cautiously maneuvering from a well-executed detour.

The first volley broke the lock of one of Calliope's guns, cut a neat under-bit in his right ear, and exploded a cartridge in his cross-belt, scorching his ribs as it burst. Feeling braced up by this unexpected tonic to his spiritual depression, Calliope executed a *fortissimo* note from his upper registers and returned the fire like an echo. The upholders of the law dodged at his flash, but a trifle too late to save one of the deputies a bullet just above the elbow and the marshal a bleeding cheek from a splinter that a ball tore from the box he had ducked behind.

And now Calliope met the enemy's tactics in kind. Choosing with a rapid eye the street from which the weakest and least accurate fire had come, he invaded it at a double-quick, abandoning the unprotected middle of the street. With rare cunning, the opposing force in that direction—one of the deputies and two of the valorous volunteers—waited, concealed by beer barrels, until Calliope had passed their retreat and then peppered him from the rear. In another moment, they were reinforced by the marshal and his other men, and then Calliope felt that in order to successfully prolong the delights of the controversy he must find some means of reducing the great odds against him. His eye fell upon a structure that seemed to hold out this promise, providing he could reach it.

Not far away was the little railroad station, its building a strong box-house, ten by twenty feet, resting upon a platform four feet above ground. Windows were in each of its walls. Something like a fort it might become to a man thus sorely pressed by superior numbers.

Calliope made a bold and rapid spurt for it, the marshal's crowd "smoking" him as he ran. He reached the haven in safety, the station agent leaving the building by a window, like a flying squirrel, as the garrison entered the door.

Patterson and his supporters halted under protection of a pile of lumber and held consultations. In the station was an unterrified desperado who was an excellent shot and carried an abundance of ammunition. For thirty yards on each side of the besieged was a stretch of bare, open ground. It was a sure thing that the man who attempted to enter that unprotected area would be stopped by one of Calliope's bullets.

The city marshal was resolved. He had decided that Calliope Catesby should no more wake the echoes of Quicksand with his strident whoop. He had so announced. Officially and personally he felt imperatively bound to put the soft pedal on that instrument of discord. It played bad tunes.

Standing near was a hand truck used in the manipulation of small freight. It stood by a shed full of sacked wool, a consignment from one of the sheep ranches. On this truck the marshal and his men piled three heavy sacks of wool. Stooping low, Buck Patterson started for Calliope's fort, slowly pushing this loaded truck before him for protection. The posse, scattering broadly, stood ready to nip the besieged in case he should show himself in an effort to repel the juggernaut of justice that was creeping upon him. Only once did Calliope make demonstration. He fired from a window and soft tufts of wool spurted from the marshal's trustworthy bulwark. The return shots from the posse pattered against the window frame of the fort. No loss resulted on either side.

The marshal was too deeply engrossed in steering his protected battleship to be aware of the approach of the morning train until he was within a few feet of the platform. The train was coming up on the other side of it. It stopped only one minute at Quicksand. What an opportunity it would offer to Calliope! He had only to step out the other door, mount the train, and away.

Abandoning his breastworks, Buck, with his gun ready, dashed up the steps and into the room, driving open the closed door with one heave of his weighty shoulder. The members of the posse heard one shot fired inside, and then there was silence.

———

At length the wounded man opened his eyes. After a blank space he again could see and hear and feel and think. Turning his eyes about, he found himself lying on a wooden bench. A tall man with a perplexed countenance, wearing a big badge with "City Marshal" engraved upon it, stood over him. A little old woman in black, with a wrinkled face and sparkling black eyes, was holding a wet handkerchief against one of his temples. He was trying to get these facts fixed in his mind and connected with past events, when the old woman began to talk.

"There now, great, big, strong man! That bullet never tetched ye! Jest skeeted along the side of your head and sort of paralysed ye for a spell. I've heerd of sech things afor! con-cussion is what they names it. Abel Wadkins used to kill squirrels that way—barkin' 'em, Abe called it. You jest been barked, sir, and you'll be all right in a little bit. Feel lots better already, don't ye! You just lay still a while longer and let me bathe your head. You don't know me, I reckon, and 'tain't surprisin' that you shouldn't. I come in on that train from Alabama to see my son. Big son, ain't he? Lands! you wouldn't hardly think he'd ever been a baby, would ye? This is my son, sir."

Half turning, the old woman looked up at the standing man, her worn face lighting with a proud and wonderful smile. She reached out one veined and calloused hand and took one of her son's. Then smiling cheerily down at the prostrate man, she continued to dip the handkerchief in the waiting-room tin washbasin and gently apply it to his temple. She had the benevolent garrulity of old age.

"I ain't seen my son before," she continued, "in eight years. One of my nephews, Elkanah Price, he's a conductor on one of them railroads, and he got me a pass to come out here. I can stay a whole week on it, and then it'll take me back again. Jest think, now, that little boy of mine has got to be a officer—a city marshal of a whole town! That's somethin' like a constable, ain't it? I never knowed he was a officer; he didn't say nothin' about it in his letters. I reckon he thought this old mother'd be skeered about the danger he was in. But, laws! I never was much of a hand to git skeered. 'Tain't no use. I heard them guns a-shootin' while I was gettin' off them cars, and I see smoke a-comin' out of the depot, but I jest walked right along. Then I see son's face lookin' out through the window. I know him at oncet. He met me at the door, and squeezed me 'most to death. And there you was, sir, a-lyin' there jest like you was dead, and I 'lowed we'd see what might be done to help sot you up."

"I think I'll sit up now," said the concussion patient. "I'm feeling pretty fair by this time."

He sat, somewhat weakly yet, leaning against the wall. He was a rugged man, big-boned and straight. His eyes, steady and keen, seemed to linger upon the face of the man standing so still above him. His look wandered often from the face he studied to the marshal's badge upon the other's breast.

"Yes, yes, you'll be all right," said the old woman, patting his arm, "if you don't get to cuttin' up agin and havin' folks shootin' at you. Son told me about you, sir, while you was layin' senseless on the floor. Don't you take it as meddlesome fer an old woman with a son as big as you to talk about it. And you mustn't hold no grudge ag'in' my son for havin' to shoot at ye. A officer has got to take up for the law—it's his duty—and them that acts bad and lives wrong has to suffer. Don't blame my son any, sir—'tain't his fault. He's always been a good boy—good when he was growin' up and kind and 'bedient and well-behaved. Won't you let me advise you, sir, not to do so no more? Be a good man and leave liquor alone and live peaceably and goodly. Keep away from bad company and work honest and sleep sweet."

The black-mittened hand of the old pleader gently touched the breast of the man she addressed. Very earnest and candid her old, worn face looked. In her rusty black dress and antique bonnet she sat, near the close of a long life, and epitomized the experience of the world. Still the man to whom she spoke gazed above her head, contemplating the silent son of the old mother.

"What does the marshal say?" he asked. "Does he believe the advice is good? Suppose the marshal speaks up and says if the talk's right?"

The tall man moved uneasily. He fingered the badge on his breast for a moment, and then he put an arm around the old woman and drew her close to him. She smiled the unchanging mother smile of three-score years and patted his big brown hand with her crooked, mittened fingers while her son spake.

"I say this," he said, looking squarely into the eyes of the other man, "that if I was in your place I'd follow it. If I was a drunken, desp'rate character, without shame or hope, I'd follow it. If I was in your place and you was in mine I'd say: 'Marshal, I'm willin' to swear if you'll give me the chance I'll quit the racket. I'll drop the tangle-foot and the gunplay, and won't play hoss no more. I'll be a good citizen and go to work and quit my foolishness. So help me God!' That's what I'd say to you if you was marshal and I was in your place."

"Hear my son talkin'," said the old woman softly. "Hear him, sir. You promise to be good and he won't do you no harm. Forty-one year ago his heart first beat ag'in' mine, and it's beat true ever since."

The other man rose to his feet, trying his limbs and stretching his muscles.

"Then," said he, "if you was in my place and said that, and I was marshal, I'd say: 'Go free, and do your best to keep your promise.'"

"Lawsy!" exclaimed the old woman, in a sudden flutter, "ef I didn't clear forget that trunk of mine! I see a man settin' it on the platform jest as I seen son's face in the window, and it went plum out of my head. There's eight jars of homemade quince jam in that trunk that I made myself. I wouldn't have nothin' happen to them jars for a red apple."

Away to the door she trotted, spry and anxious, and then Calliope Catesby spoke out to Buck Patterson:

"I just couldn't help it, Buck. I seen her through the window a-comin' in. She had never heard a word 'bout my tough ways. I didn't have the nerve to let her know I was a worthless cuss bein' hunted down by the community. There you was lyin' where my shot laid you, like you was dead. The idea struck me sudden, and I just took your badge off and fastened it onto myself, and I fastened my reputation onto you. I told her I was the marshal and you was a holy terror. You can take your badge back now, Buck."

With shaking fingers, Calliope began to unfasten the disc of metal from his shirt.

"Easy there!" said Buck Patterson. "You keep that badge right where it is, Calliope Catesby. Don't you dare to take it off till the day your mother leaves this town. You'll be city marshal of Quicksand as long as she's here to know it. After I stir around town a bit and put 'em on, I'll guarantee that nobody won't give the thing away to her. And say, you leather-headed, rip-roarin', low-down son of a locoed cyclone, you follow that advice she give me! I'm goin' to take some of it myself, too."

"Buck," said Calliope feelingly, "ef I don't I hope I may—"

"Shut up," said Buck. "She's a-comin' back."

Long Ride Back

By Ed Gorman

SOON AS I SNUCK into his campsite and kicked him in the leg so he'd jerk up from his blanket, I brought down the stock of my single-shot .40–90 Sharps and did some real damage to his teeth.

He was swearing and crying all the time I got him in handcuffs, spraying blood that looked black in the dawn flames of the fading campfire.

In the dewy grass, in the hard frosty cold of the September morning, the white birches just now starting to gleam in the early sunlight, I got the Kid's roan saddled and then went back for the Kid himself.

"I ain't scared of you," he said, talking around his busted teeth and bloody tongue.

"Well, that makes us even. I ain't scared of you, either."

I dragged him over to the horse, got him in the saddle, and then took a two-foot piece of rawhide and lashed him to the horn.

"You sonofabitch," the Kid said. He said that a lot.

Then I was up in my own saddle and we headed back to town. It was a long day's ride.

———

"They'll be braggin' about ya, I suppose, over to the saloon, I mean," the Kid said a little later, as we moved steadily along the stage road.

"I don't pay attention to stuff like that."

"How the big brave sheriff went out and captured the Kid all by his lonesome."

I ain't scared of you.

"Why don't you be quiet for a while?"

"Yessir. All by his lonesome. And you know how many murder counts are on the Kid's head? Why, three of them in Nebraska alone. And two more right here in Kansas. Why, even the James Boys walked wide of the Kid—and then here's this hick sheriff capturin' him all by hisself. What a hero."

This time I didn't ask him.

I leaned over and backhanded him so hard, he started to slide off his saddle. Through his pain and blood, he started calling me names again.

It went like that most of the morning, him starting up with his ugly tongue and me quieting him down with the back of my hand.

At least the countryside was pretty, autumn blazing in the hills surrounding this dusty valley, chicken hawks arcing against the soft blue sky.

Then he said, "You goin' to be there when they hang me?"

I shrugged.

"When they put the rope around my neck and the hood over my face and give the nod to the hangman?"

I said nothing. I rode. Nice and steady. Nice and easy.

"Oh, you're a fine one, you are," the Kid said. "A fine one."

Around noon, the sun very high and hot, I stopped at a fast blue creek and gave the horses water and me and the Kid some jerky.

I ate mine. The Kid spit his out. Right in my face.

Then we were up and riding again.

"You sonofabitch," the Kid said. There was so much anger in him, it never seemed to wane at all.

I sighed. "There's nothing to say, Kid."

"There's plenty to say and you know it."

"In three years you killed six people, two of them women, and all so you could get yourself some easy money from banks. There's not one goddamned thing to add to that. Not one goddamned thing." Now it was me who was angry.

"You sonofabitch," he said, "I'm your son. Don't that mean anything?"

"Yeah, Karl, it means plenty. It means I had to watch your mother die a slow death of shame and heartbreak. And it means you put me in a position I didn't ask for—you shot a man in cold blood in my jurisdiction. So I had to come after you. I didn't want to—I prayed you'd be smart enough to get out of my territory before I found you. But you weren't smart at all. You figured I'd let you go." I looked down at the silver star on my leather vest. "But I couldn't, Karl. I just couldn't."

He started crying, then, and I wanted to say something or do something to comfort him but I didn't know what.

I just listened to the owls in the woods and rode on, with my own son next to me in handcuffs, toward the town that a hanging judge named Coughlin visited seven times a year, a town where the citizens turned hangings into civic events, complete with parades and picnics after.

"You really gonna let 'em hang me, Pa?" Karl said after a while, still crying, and sounding young and scared now. "You really gonna let 'em hang me?"

I didn't say anything. There was just the soughing wind.

"Ma woulda let me go if she was here. You know she would."

I just rode on, closer, ever closer to town. Three more hours. To make my mind up. To be sure.

"Pa, you can't let 'em hang me, you can't." He was crying again.

And then I realized that I was crying, too, as we rode on closer and closer and closer to where men with singing saws and blunt hard hammers and silver shining nails waited for another life to place on the altar of the scaffold.

"You gotta let me go, Pa, you just gotta," Karl said.

Three more hours and, one way or another, it would all be over. Maybe I would change my mind, maybe not. We rode on toward the dusty autumn hills.

Home on the Range

By Brewster Higley

Oh, give me a home where the buffalo roam,
Where the deer and the antelope play.
Where seldom is heard a discouraging word,
And the skies are not cloudy all day.

Home, home on the range,
Where the deer and the antelope play.
Where seldom is heard a discouraging word,
And the skies are not cloudy all day.

Where the air is so pure, the zephyrs so free,
The breezes so balmy and light.
That I would not exchange my home on the range
For all of the cities so bright.

Home, home on the range,
Where the deer and the antelope play.
Where seldom is heard a discouraging word,
And the skies are not cloudy all day.

How often at night when the heavens are bright,
With the light from the glittering stars.
Here I stood there amazed, and asked as I gazed,
If their glory exceeds that of ours.

Where the buffalo roam.

Home, home on the range,
Where the deer and the antelope play.
Where seldom is heard a discouraging word,
And the skies are not cloudy all day.

I love the wild flowers in this dear land of ours,
And the curlew I love to hear scream.
I love the wild rocks and the antelope flocks,
That graze on the mountaintops green.

Home, home on the range,
Where the deer and the antelope play.
Where seldom is heard a discouraging word,
And the skies are not cloudy all day.

Credits

SPECIAL THANKS to Cheryl Blanchard and Alice Wand, librarians at the Paine Memorial Free Library in Willsboro, New York, for their help in searching for many more stories than could be included in this volume.

Thanks, too, to Cara Moser for her photographic skills in helping the illustrator invent some of these images. And a very special thanks to the many photographers, now dead and unknown, who documented life in the West and who supplied the illustrator with a great deal of accurate information. And thanks to the various filmmakers whose films have been freely quoted.